The Sins of the Father…
and of the Son

James A. Naughton

ISBN: 1514653990
ISBN-13: 9781514653999

DEDICATION

For my wife, Kay, and my children, Elizabeth, Matthew and Ellen. For so many years, you have been my motivation to be the best that I can be, no matter what my endeavors. I hope *The Sins of the Father... and of the Son* measures up.

The author is indebted to Bradford Angier and his book, *Skills for Taming the Wilds*.

*For the sins of the fathers, you, though guiltless,
must suffer.*

Horace
Odes III

*When all its work is done, the lie shall rot;
The truth is great, and shall prevail
When none cares whether it prevail or not.*

Magna est Veritas
Coventry Patmore

.

*The souls of all who have ever lived
dwell in the woods. And you and I?
We are but intruders there, come to
learn the truths that only the dead
can tell. I hear their voices in the
wind through the leaves in the night,
in the rush of clear-running streams
in the dawn's lingering mist.
Speaking to me... To you... To any
who enter there. But one must devote
a lifetime of hard listening—of
learning to listen with the heart—to
ever hope of deciphering the truths
from those wandering souls.*

1935
DAY ONE

1

He leaned forward and touched the ridge of bone with his fingertips. "My god, David Haph, what the christ have you done to yourself?" Grimacing, he went back hard on his hands and closed his eyes against the pain. The sun above the humped mountains across the valley glowed orange and heatless through his eyelids.

This couldn't have happened. What he was seeing had to be a lie. Things like this just didn't happen to him.

He opened his eyes.

"Look at it, you dumb bastard. If you think that's not broken…"

He looked at his left leg. The bone made a peak under his trousers halfway up his shin.

He sat on a wide ledge, legs straight out. Now he walked his hands back four short steps and looked around. Behind him, a wall of rock rose as high as a house. The ledge where he sat was part of this same cliff face, but it was covered with brown leaves and dark soil redolent with eons of decay. He surveyed the facing valley, turning his head left to right to take in the full sweep of rolling mountains. They seemed to undulate away from him forever. The wilderness was skeletal, an intricate weave of trunks and shadow in the harsh glow of February sunlight. To either side of the ledge, the trees were myriad and deep, jutting out of their own shadows. In front of him, though, only the treetops peeked above the rim of the ledge. There the trees dropped away with the mountainside, only to rear again across the valley, thick and diminutive, standing rigid on the rolling flanks like hairs on the back of a hissing cat.

The trees blanketed the mountains as far down the valley as he could see.

He shook his head and snorted mirthlessly.

It could have been worse, he supposed. His leg had taken the brunt of it. What if his chest had hit first? He'd be dead now; he did not doubt it. But what in hell would he do now?

He touched a tender area on his chest under left his arm.

Well, no broken ribs, anyway. And he had his head again... though a lot of good it would do him. He'd freeze to death. Maybe not tonight... but tomorrow night, or the night after. The matches would run out, and he had nothing for the cold except this wool shirt and sheepskin vest. Or maybe he'd really luck out and the gangrene would get him. Yeah, that was more like it. Three or four days of this lovely goddamn pain before his leg rotted off. Then his carcass would proclaim to anyone who found him: *Final resting place of David Haph, the dumb bastard his old man always said he was.* And he could just hear him: 'Just set the son of a bitch and get done with it. I ain't waitin' all day.' He'd say it just like that, wouldn't he—like there wasn't any more to it than gutting a fish. And he'd answer him back: For christ's sake, Pa, it's broken clear in half. I could use a little help. And then: 'Help! I'll give you a little help. You got your ass into this mess. Now you can just get it out again, too.'

He blinked once and fluttered his eyelids. He was aware of the cold again, aware of the sun perched above the mountaintops.

Who in hell was he kidding? In his whole life he never talked back to him. And the son of a bitch would be right this time. Only some greenhorn falls off a ledge while taking off his coat. "Jesus, David." He hammered the ground with his fist, then drew his shirtsleeve across his forehead and beard. When he exhaled, his breath streamed white from his nostrils.

"Well, David," he whispered, "it might have been better if the woods killed you thirty years ago." He'd like to think he cheated the woods that day, but he knew better. Everyone knew his old man could track anything, even a five-year-old boy that was half as smart as any forest animal and twice as unpredictable. His old man made sure he left him out there long enough, though... a day and a night and most of another day. Made sure he was good and scared. And why? Because he blamed him for killing his precious Ellie. What kind of a man lets a child think he killed his own mother?

The clearing darkened, and he started, then watched a cloud sliding in front of the sun. The mountains across the valley darkened, too, until they looked depthless and without detail. Only the birches were distinct, etched like white capillaries on bruise-colored skin.

He listened hard for a moment, but the wilderness was silent, and it felt as if the silence were moving into him, enormous and empty. The beating of his heart, so panicked moments after his fall, seemed lost now, beating deep within the emptiness.

Well, a broken leg didn't have to me mean a death sentence. He didn't intend to go out like this. He'd have to set the bone. He didn't need to look to know it had ripped through the skin. If he saw how bad it was, he might lose his nerve.

He thought about setting the bone, about feeling it pull back through the skin and lock against the stump of his upper shin. He shuddered.

And what about after that? What about gathering wood? How would he do that... by crawling around on his belly like snake?

He chuckled humorlessly and swallowed.

Well, his old man might mock him, but that didn't mean he'd give the bastard the satisfaction of seeing him quit. He screwed up—royally for sure—but he hadn't given up. Not yet.

To his far right, in close to the rock wall that ran the full width of the ledge, a fallen tree pointed up the valley. Halfway up its trunk, two rocks supported it, leaving space above the ground.

He could light his fire there. The trunk would draw the smoke and keep it from chasing him all night. He wasn't in any shape for that. No mood, either.

Closer to him, two rocks jutted at an angle that formed a 'V' between. He could see other rocks and limbs in the clearing, many small enough for him to handle for firewood. Larger limbs he would have to chop up. He felt for the hatchet on his right hip. It was there, its leather scabbard fastened.

He went flat to the ground and rolled onto his right side. Feeling the sheath on his left hip, he unsnapped it and withdrew his knife by its bone handle. He brought the yellowed handle close and rubbed his thumb against it, feeling its ridges and grooves.

It felt so hard. Like rock. How could anything that hard have broken? Or was the bone in his leg different because it was living bone and this was dead?

Maybe he'd shouldn't use the knife. Why chance breaking the blade?

He did not sheathe the knife. Instead, he held it blade upward in his left hand and set his right forearm on the ground and, pushing with his right foot, pulled himself forward. The pain scalded in his shin, and he gasped and stopped.

A few seconds later he dragged himself forward again, three times, quickly. But the leaves he pushed against were slick on their undersides. He felt his right foot slip and then glance off the broken bone. With a scream, he slammed his fist into his forehead and stiffened. He pulled an agonized breath into his throat and rolled onto his back and then quickly onto his right side again. Then he screamed again and held himself rigid.

In awhile, he could draw breath. The cold air seethed through his teeth in a shaking, sibilant sucking. He rolled onto his butt and pushed himself up.

Sweet jesus. He should have broken his neck. How did he think he was going to set that?

He looked at the peak pressing against his gray wool trousers.

'You don't think about it; you just do it.'

"Oh, go fuck yourself, Jacob. This is what I think of that."

He set the knife against his wrist and pressed the blade. Then he pressed harder, watching the blade as it glinted in the sunlight. But then he eased.

No, that took more guts than he had. He didn't want to go out scared to death like his old man, though. What a day. It was so hot dying seemed like a half-sensible thing to do. But there was his old man, out in the sun, splitting wood like Hell had an urgent need for a delivery.

What he remembered clearest, though, was the sound. The thunk and then the crack of the ax. And the clatter the wood made when it fell. A dry, hard sound. And then the thunk when his old man set another log on the stump. It seemed to pick at him that day, like the heat, just going on and on without ever changing. Crack—clatter—thunk.

He wasn't watching his old man when it happened. He was piling wood near the back steps. Didn't have strength enough to swing an ax. Least that's what his old man told him. When he was sixteen maybe, but not fifteen. He was still a boy.

He was bent over, halfway to setting down another piece, when he heard the whacking suddenly stop off and his old man make that funny sound. And for a minute there was no sound, and he just stayed like he was, holding that piece of wood.

The quiet raised all the hairs on his body. It seemed like such a long time that he waited for the whacking to start up again. But there was just the quiet humming in his ears.

It wasn't until his old man croaked his name, "David!" that he moved. It sounded so awful, with the fear making his father's voice rise at the end. And then he whirled and looked. He didn't see all of his father at first, just pieces—first his face, and not even his whole face but just his eyes, round and so scared looking, and then his father's hand against his forehead, and then his mouth because it was moving, trying to form words, but just chewing the air, and then back to his eyes. He couldn't keep from looking. Maybe because it was one of the few times he'd seen anything there, any emotion, even if it was just fear. So they went on looking at each other until his old man blurted: "David! I can't..."

Whatever it was, he didn't finish. He let go of the ax and came tottering forward with his arm all stretched out, grasping at just the air, his body a bright apparition, looking like the very devil himself. And then he went down, falling into the dirt like a tree falls, not able to slow or brace himself. And when he hit, his black hat came off and rolled on its brim before it settled in the dust.

And then it was like the earth had sucked all sound out of the world. It felt like nothing would ever move again. So he was surprised to see his old man's head come up, shaking—his eyebrows and the stubble on his cheeks and chin all covered with dust, and his face hollow, with the eyes staring out like two animals scared near to death.

Still he couldn't move; he could only look back, had to look back, like he was in wonder with the fear.

It wasn't until he saw the welling in his old man's eyes that he realized he was begging for him to come, and then he understood.

The feeling changed fast. He remembered the heat, how the hollowness inside him all of a sudden got hot, with his heart banging away in the middle. And he could remember thinking: Damn him! God damn him to hell! He's doing it to me, too!

And then his old man called out. Just a whisper, a gasp. But it got him running.

He raced to him and stopped. But he could not stop the feeling that was pushing down, down inside him...

"No!"

He shook his head violently, stopped, then shook it violently again. He drew his shirtsleeve across his brow and shook his head a third time. He could see his quick breaths puffing into the cold air, and then he realized that his skin felt clammy, like the leaves beneath him.

Look; he was sweating. Just what he needed. Get goddamn hypothermia on top of everything else.

He looked at the peak pushing against his trousers.

Hell, even if he set that, he couldn't walk out on it. Not the two or so miles between him and Randolph Falls.

"Randolph Falls." He snorted. Might as well be on the other side of the world. Hell, there wasn't much there anyway. Except the tannery. If he got close enough, maybe he could smell his way out.

He turned onto his stomach and crawled again, digging his right toe in and pulling himself up to his hands, each time smelling their rank, earth smell. He moved slowly, making sure of his toehold. After covering ten yards or so, he stopped. The pain was molten in his leg.

Stay put. Isn't that what you were supposed to do? Easier to find a man if he stayed put. But who in hell was there to look for him? Only Dick knew he was out here, and would he blow into Randolph Falls tomorrow like he was supposed to? And would he look?

He was dreaming. It could take a week maybe longer to find him. By then he'd be belly up like a fish in a bucket. Things just kept getting better and better.

Soon he had crawled to one of the limbs near the jutting 'V' rocks. Like the other limbs in the clearing, this one had fallen from the trees atop the cliff.

His breathing was rapid and shallow as he slipped the knife into its sheath. He raised the limb like the mast of a sailboat and leaned his weight on one branch. It broke, snapping like a derringer shot into the solitude. He broke off another and let the limb topple away and stripped the branches and broke them against the rocks. He drew his good leg up to his chest and held the branches along the shin.

They'll do, he thought.

As he patted his face on his sleeve, he watched two crows fly overhead. Beyond the ledge, they cawed to each other. Then, wings quiet, they dipped toward the valley, but their cawing rang through the solitude long after they disappeared.

They would have stopped to give him a try if he'd been a bit unluckier. Probably telling each other to come back and look for that one in a day or two.

The cawing faded, and he shuddered as the silence welled out of the wilderness again. Except for a stand of pine or spruce among the hardwoods, nothing appeared to be alive. Yet, as always, he sensed something in the silence. It had a feeling, like the air had a coldness, only less palpable, bigger, as if some presence had hushed itself within the infinite sprawl of trees, waiting for movement, listening for any sound.

A chill rattled inside him.

Maybe it was just the woods. Maybe something this big and this old took on its own being after a time. Or maybe it was the souls his old man talked about. Whatever, he had felt it in the woods for as long as he could remember.

He drew the limb closer, then set it on its end and walked his hands up the shaft and pulled himself onto his right foot, drawing a gasp into his throat when his left leg lifted free. He looked at the sun.

It would be dark in a couple of hours, and there would be no moon tonight. He wouldn't have any light after sun set. Not good.

It wouldn't do any good just to splint it, would it? He looked at his leg. No. That was stupid.

"Do it the right way, David."

He'd scream like an old woman, though. And what if the bone didn't set? The gangrene didn't care what he did to the bone. It cared only about the blood, and there was nothing he could do for that if he didn't set it right.

He looked at the mountains and thought about how far he'd have to hobble on one leg. Distance was multiplied in the woods, even on two good legs, but distance was meaningless now. It felt like the wilderness had suddenly expanded exponentially. One mile was the end of the world. Two miles... down and up mountains on one leg... Christ, that was the end of the universe.

The purple mountains rolled on forever. He shook his head. How puny, how meaningless, he felt. Not even his old man could make him feel any worse.

"Stop whining and get it over with. You don't have a choice."

He walked his hands up the limb, level with his eyes, then vaulted forward. As he circled the rocks, a lightness wafted into his head and, by the time he reached the far side, drops of sweat were stinging his eyes, making the trees look half-liquid in the sunlight.

He patted his eyes on his sleeve, and the trees became brown and hard again. Then he lowered himself onto the rocks and dropped the limb on the other side before easing his body over. As soon as his rump hit the ground, he catapulted backward, and then he laid still, clenching his breath. He could feel sweat beading on his forehead.

Pushing himself into a sitting position, he leaned forward and gripped his leg just below the break. His hands shook as he lifted it and set the boot between the 'V' in the rocks. Then he went flat against the ground and, with his right foot, hammered gently on the boot, driving the toe to his left and wedging his ankle to provide an unmovable anchor.

He closed his eyes, waiting for the fire in his leg to smolder.

He'd have to do it on the first try. He couldn't stand to do it a second time.

He placed his right foot squarely against the rightmost rock, then walked himself into a sitting position with his hands. His heart was beating rapidly, and he tasted a brininess in his mouth. He concentrated on pushing, but his right leg remained bent.

Come one, come on. Push.

He stared at his leg, as if willing it to straighten. He hated this feeling, like there was something alive inside, clawing to get out.

'Can't help being scared. Any man would be scared.'

"Up yours, Jacob."

Suddenly, his right leg locked, and he pushed against the rock. His right side shuddered, but the sensation was devoured by the chewing in his left leg. He groaned and pulled the sound into himself. A moment later, he heard his voice screaming. It was inside his head at first, but then exploded out, as if the wilderness itself were bellowing in revulsion.

He bore down harder, but when he could not force the bone to move, he pushed down on it with his hands. He arched his body farther right, trying to stretch his leg, to will the bone to move back through the skin. He gulped breath, half hearing the screaming stop an instant. Again, he pushed against the bone with his hands, once, hard, and he felt it move. He barely sensed the movement with his hands, but inside his leg, he was sure he had felt the severed bone scrape against the stump below his knee.

Then he could not will himself to sit upright any longer. He shot back, the pain so molten in his shin he could see it inside his closed eyes, blinding. His eyes bulged against his eyelids as he dug his fingers into the half-frozen soil and strained to move the bone. A dizziness rushed into his head, and his eyes shot open. He raised his head, straining to look at the rocks, the trees. Everything swirled—stopped— swirled again. Then he felt his head wobble, and the sky was dark—darker—gone.

August 1905

His aunt and uncle were out beyond the tall grass, the swipes of their badminton rackets coming to him across the field in much the same way as their laughter—in flashes, quick and bright.

He was pulling clumps of grass and hurling them against the ground because she had left him there, under the tree, with his father. She wasn't his mother, he knew that, but she looked just like his mother.

He looked at his father. He was dressed in the blue overalls and dingy white undershirt that he always wore, his lank, almost gaunt, body slumped against the tree, black hat pulled over his eyes. His breathing was slow and shallow.

It was just as he was turning his eyes away that he saw it—something small and bright fluttering against the trees before it disappeared into the grass.

He started after it, his feet folding the tall grass white in the sunlight as he tried to steal past his father. And he made it farther than he expected, had, in fact, reached his uncle's automobile and was moving past the second of the yellow-spoked wheels before his father's voice stopped him.

"Don't you go nowhere far. I told you to keep set awhile."

"Yes, Pa."

He looked back, but the other had not even raised the hat from his eyes. Then he went on, up to the edge of the woods. He did not intend to enter, only to look for the bright thing. The woods were dark, like the woods around their farm. Sometimes he would hide along the fringe when his father was working near the house, preventing him from stealing to the hill where his mother was buried and talking to her.

So it seemed familiar to him. He looked down then, intending to resume his search when, suddenly, it fluttered up before his face—a yellow and black butterfly. He snatched at it—once—twice—but it floated out of reach into the woods, and, before there was time even to recall his father's words, he was chasing it, reaching for it as it flickered just beyond his fingers. On he pursued it, but the butterfly remained out of reach, fluttering tauntingly until, at the base of a large sycamore, it suddenly floated upward and lighted on a leaf, where its wings settled into an easy folding and unfolding, as if it were breathing, as if it were trying to catch its breath just as he was trying to catch his.

It was when his breathing was quiet that he heard, faintly, a roaring through the trees. He gave the butterfly one last look, then ran off to find the sound.

It did not take long to reach the stream. It surged between two steep banks, the sunlight falling in blotches here and there on its few quiet pools. But he had no sooner reached the bank and looked down, when the earth gave way beneath his feet and, before he could stop himself, he was sliding down the too-steep bank. Up the water came, so fast. In went his feet, the water surging around his ankles.

Even as he scrambled onto the bank, the thought was in his head: Pa... He'll hit me. When he sees, he'll hit me bad.

And so he ran, first along the bank, until the land flattened, and then away from the stream and into the woods. He ran until his lungs could no longer catch air. There were only two sounds after that—the bellows of his own urgent panting and the squashing of his shoes as he slowed to a walk. He could see brown foam oozing around the soles with each step.

It was not until he had caught his breath that he realized it: He had no idea where he was. And instantly, rising out of the center of his ballooning panic, he sensed it for the first time—that something was watching him. It rose into his awareness as a fish rises from the depths of a lake, at first nearly imperceptible, and then rushing up to become fully formed and real.

He held his breath, listening, and the forest seemed to stop breathing, too. But there was no sound, just the dim and sultry gloom of summer woods.

And then he sensed that it was behind him, and so he ran again, whimpering and looking over his shoulder. He ran and ran deeper into the woods.

He never saw what tripped him. All he remembered was hurtling through the air and the rock that rushed up, crushing the right side of his forehead.

When he opened his eyes, the forest was darker. It soared above him like an enormous leather wing, the light dying from the specks of sky visible through the leaves.

The rock under him was sticky with his blood, and his head throbbed so, he dared not move. So he listened in the quiet darkness and waited. And then it was there again—that sense that something was watching him.

So he could only lie there and wait for it, with his fear wound up tight inside. Gradually, the light faded, and the forest lost detail, deepening first to charcoal and finally to black.

Even if he could not move, his eyes still could. They darted in the direction of any sound. He did not scream, not even later when he heard a rustling, so loud, he knew it was not his imagination. It came toward him from behind, and because he was just five, just a child, what he pictured was not any familiar forest animal—squirrel, or chipmunk, or rabbit—but something enormous and shaggy.

Then it stopped. He could feel his heart clamoring against his ribs. Did it know he was there?

The next sound was its claws ripping at a log. He moaned, sucking the sound in at first in a long shuddering breath before letting it out again.

There was a rustling then, like wind in the trees. It's heard me! he told himself. It's coming for me!

But it did not. The forest became still again, black and fathomless.

The sounds continued all night, and each time his heart leapt against his ribs, and he tried not to moan.

It went on until there was light again through the morning mist, and the mist changed from blue, to gray, to white, and finally vaporized like steam and the trees condensed out of it, black and hard.

For hours, it did not change. Only the light filtering through the leaves changed, becoming stronger, slowly increasing the angle of its descent. Now it came lance-like through the holes between the leaves and broke on the ground here, and there, and there, but the shafts were all far away so, where he was lying, it was dark, surrounded by bars of light.

He raised his head and probed the darkness, but he saw only tree trunks, countless and black, and branches heavy with leaves.

"D-a-a-a-a-v-i-i-i-d."

The voice drifted to him, like the voice of a dying man, or

of one already dead.

He struggled to rise, his hands crumpling the leaves from the ground. He could feel the cold, dead-fish feel of their undersides. Then he caught a flicker in the gloom, gone when he looked back.

"D-a-a-a-a-v-i-i-i-d."

The voice seemed to come from all around him, sourceless.

"Here!" he called. His eyes darted. "Here!"

"D-a-a-a-a-v-i-i-i-d."

He saw a figure then. It did not come directly toward him, but closer nonetheless, until it entered one of the bars of light and stopped. He could see clearly now—a tall man, wiry, dressed in blue bib overalls, his black hat riding just above the eyes.

"Father."

When their eyes met, he saw a smile flicker in the murk beneath the hat. It was not a smile of gladness or recognition, just quick. "There you are," his father said without emotion.

He moved forward. His thin body went black, then bright, then black again as he passed through a bar of light. Finally, he was standing over him.

"Pa." He reached up, but the other did not move. He saw the quick, bright smile again. His father's face hardened. "I hope you learned a lesson from this, boy. Looks like you banged yourself up pretty good." Then his father leaned forward, reaching for him. He shut his eyes and felt the cold, branch-like fingers go beneath him, and he started to cry.

"It's over. Stop your crying," his father said. The voice was like his touch, without any trace of affection. He held him with the same degree of caring with which he'd seen him hold a bag of feed.

"I said, stop crying."

He saw shadows move beyond his father's shoulder, beyond the bars of light. Men. The trees spat them into the light—four... eight... more.

"Found him, Jacob?" one man said.

"Yeah, I found him."

"What are you raising there, running off and pulling a stunt like this?" This was a man with a black beard and hair, and a mouth that was just a slit of yellow showing through the black.

"He knew better," his father answered. "Told him to stay put, but he don't listen. Ain't ever learned to listen."

A gaunt, old man with wild hair approached. The man gently placed one hand on his shoulder. "Son, you're lucky you got him for an old man. Not sure anyone else could have found you."

Then his uncle materialized from nowhere. He was wearing a long canvas duster. "Lord, Jacob, he's hurt. His head's bleeding."

"Yeah, we best get that tended to right off." Then to him: "It hurt much, boy? How'd you do that to yourself?"

"Yes, it hurts, Pa. It hurts awful. I fell running 'cause I was so scared."

"I know, I know," his father said. "But it's over now. There ain't nothing to be scared of. But next time I tell you to stay put, what are you gonna do?"

"Stay put," he answered bitterly. Then he squirmed in his father's arms, but his father tightened his grip. "I want mama," he cried, but when his father's hold did not loosen, he buried his face in his father's bony shoulder and cried.

Behind his closed eyes, he could see his mother, and hear her, too: "David! David! They found you!"

Yes, he wanted to answer. Found, Mother. He pictured her in the tall grass of the field behind their house. Her face was white with sunlight, and he could see the blueness of her eyes. Her arms were open. He wanted so much for her to hold him.

"Okay, boys," his father said. "Let's get him to the doc. Our work's done here."

And with that, his mother vanished, and he never felt more alone.

2

He bolted upright, calling her name out of his unconsciousness, "Carrie." An explosion of pain jolted him rigid. Then he saw his left foot wedged between the rocks.

He eased himself back until he felt the cold ground beneath him. A dull aching pounded in his head.

For awhile, he was quiet, and the pounding receded, and the fire in his leg diminished.

He closed his eyes. From both sides of the clearing, the squawking and chirping of jays and sparrows, and now and then the call of a chickadee, rang from the barren trees.

Blinking, he opened his eyes and looked into the sky. It was deep blue, and the sun had swung farther to his right and lower and was fixed above the dark mountains across the valley.

The birds clamored and flapped in the trees.

Roosting, he told himself. Or soon anyway. He rolled his head.

He'd passed out, damn him. At best there were two hours of daylight left. Probably less.

He repositioned his head, trying to make the throbbing settle, and he shivered. His fingers were numb, and he slid them under his vest and into his armpits, and he felt his shirt press against him, damp with cold perspiration.

And then a pool of aching welled into him, and the old dead

emptiness from long ago was in him once more.

He was never going to shed her, was he? She could pop up at the damnedest times. Not every night anymore. But when something was working at him. Then, often as not, she was there. Not to stay... but as if to remind him of her flight all those years ago.

Wilkey... James Everston Wilkey... Now there was a first-rate asshole for you. He was engaged to her. Then he abandoned her. Told her there was another woman. But David Haph knew there was some other reason. He just didn't know what.

He remembered the day Wilkey left. How she cried. How she kept saying over and over: 'You are life to me. Life to me.' Wilkey told her that, and who knows what other nonsense. What he remembered clearest, though, was how good it felt to hold her. In the four years he'd known her, he never held her until that moment. It sounded stupid, but that was the closest he ever got to heaven in this life. And he could remember thinking that if it could only go on like that, just holding her, he wouldn't want any more out of life. But she didn't know that he loved her. Not then. He was sorry about her pain, but he was glad, too, if he was honest. Not glad... Hopeful maybe. Because it meant he might have a chance... not right then, but someday.

He was the one she turned to. It was her pain that finally gave him the guts to tell her how he felt. In the park in Bennington. He knew she didn't love him, but he wanted her to know that someone loved her, that she wasn't beyond love even if it was only his. How could he not love her? She'd given him back his life, pulled him back into the world.

Thinking about it now... Up to that moment, his love for her had been controllable. As long as he hadn't told her. That's because there wasn't any hope, any expectation, that she could ever feel the same.

But saying three words changed that. It let the proverbial genie out of the bottle, and the genie demanded to be satisfied. Three words created the hope, and hope is the very devil itself. Hope is the demon that keeps your heart suffering long after your mind told you that a thing is impossible.

Their relationship changed then. How intense it got; he got. Then the real pain started. It was more than just desperation to have her return the feeling. It was like everything he ever felt for her, had kept hidden for four years, suddenly had to burst out of him in four minutes, four seconds.

And she did respond. Not with love. "Love is a word I don't like to use." She said that. But it was like the world was made anew and everything assumed a new intensity. Suddenly, he needed to share everything, things he had never shared with anyone. He wanted to give himself to her—his heart, his thoughts, his mind, his body—anything she wanted. It wasn't that he expected the same. But if she couldn't love him, he hoped at least that she would let him go on being with her.

Strange that what had been so painful seemed so wonderful now. And so sad. Those few short weeks. That's all it was. Then she was gone. One letter telling him the same things that they talked about in the final days: she needed time; he was suffering and she knew he would not ask her to bear that burden knowing it would crush her; he had a lot of work to do before he found what he was looking for in her. And so many other things. But never saying that she wasn't coming back, that he wasn't going to hear from her ever again. And her bitch of a sister, refusing to tell him where she was so he could write to her. She seemed to actually enjoy telling him that Carrie didn't want to hear from him, not then, not ever. But he couldn't believe that. Not until it had gone on so long even he had no choice but to accept it.

But why had she done that? How could she do that?

She must have felt something. She'd taken him into her life, let him get closer to her than he had ever been to anyone then or since, and he knew what he thought about that. When you let someone into your life, you took on an obligation.

"So, damn you, Carolyn Worthy, what about your obligation to me? What about that?"

s eyes and expelled his breath.

ιe the worst thing in the world to him. She let him

ght feel like to be whole, and then she took it away.

why... Maybe then he could finally get shed of her.

A screaming erupted from the trees. He could see a crow perched near the top of an oak. Two jays dove at it, trying to drive it off. They darted, screaming, and the crow dodged and cawed and then, flapping, hopped to a lower branch and finally leapt from the tree, wings laboring to lift it. The jays pursued, harassing the larger bird until it was out over the valley. He watched the crow's slow and graceless retreat as it winged into the dying day

His skull throbbed, and he cursed the birds and rested his head on the ground.

"Let them be," he muttered. They'd shut up when it got dark. For them, darkness meant safety. For him, it meant more cold, and he already had enough.

He moved his fingers under his arms and pushed against his ribs, but no matter how tightly he pressed with his arms, he could not get the warmth back in his fingers. He shivered and looked at the trees and their lengthening shadows.

What about his leg? He supposed looking was the only way to tell.

With his right arm, he pushed himself up and leaned forward. His leg seethed. He inched his trouser up, but when he saw his leg, he gasped and turned his head away.

His leg was already black, and it was swollen, like a sausage in its casing. Halfway up his shin, there was an oblong bruise bigger than his fist, and from its center, a jagged ridge of bone protruded. The wound was moist with blood, and there was drying blood on his shin and calf. The bone had moved. It was better; but he had failed to set it.

"Good jesus," he whispered. He hadn't wanted to believe it was that bad. Now what? Maybe it was the swelling that made it look so bad. There was bound to be swelling. He'd splint it. That might keep the bone from moving. He'd splint it, and he'd be all right. He mustn't lose his head was all.

Still, his heart continued to race as he worked his trouser leg down. He looked at the sun. It was orange and flat, as if shining through a hole punched in the sky. Four fingers of sky remained between it and the mountaintop.

When the bone was concealed, he braced himself against the pain and worked his right foot under his wedged boot and pried it free of the rocks. Then he lifted his leg in his hands and, stifling a cry, swiveled and set it on the ground.

He started to remove the red laces from his boots, but his hands were red and ached with cold, and he cupped them and blew on them and rubbed them together briskly. Then he removed the laces.

He used his knife to cut a short length from each lace, which he fastened through the top eyelets of his boots. Then he retrieved the branches he had broken earlier and bound them along his shin with the remaining lace, the pain in his leg rising to a shriek until he finished and eased himself back. He slid his hands beneath the sheepskin vest and under his arms.

It wasn't the best splint, but he couldn't chance tying it too tightly. The blood was having enough trouble without him cutting off the circulation. He'd see. In a while there would be a little numbness and he'd be able to think better. But already he was thinking well and clearly. If he dragged the boot off, he'd never get it on again. And now that wouldn't be a problem.

That was the whole thing. Thinking well and clearly. That was all and he'd get out of this.

He looked across the valley, marking once more the progress of the sinking sun. High above, a few thin clouds hung immobile, like shreds of hair.

His luck wasn't all bad. On a north-facing slope, the sun would be gone now, and he'd be colder than he was. The sun was always in the southern sky in winter. That's what he needed now; things he could count on. But not luck. What was it that Dick had said? Luck was like a whore. For awhile she might play all the games with you that you wanted, but in the end, she just wound up screwing you.

What he wouldn't give to see him walk out of the trees.

He closed his eyes against the sun's heatless light.

The day still hadn't come that he'd been able to talk to him. At least not about things he'd been able to tell Carrie. He wasn't sure why exactly. For sure, Dick was the best soul he'd ever met in his life. And if there was anyone who could teach you to laugh... But Dick could also never leave well enough alone, and he just didn't like the way he was always probing. Always trying to figure out why David Haph was like he was. He always tried to be honest with Dick, though. And if he couldn't be honest, he didn't say anything. Carrie was the only one he ever allowed inside, and honesty drove her out of his life. Maybe that was why he never talked to Dick. Maybe he was afraid of driving him out, too. Or of letting him get too close.

He closed his eyes, then opened them. Across the valley, the blue-purple of the north-facing mountain was deepening with the dying day. He shuddered.

Enough. Dick and Carrie weren't going to light a fire for him.

Sliding his hands from under his arms and bunching them into fists to conserve warmth, he crawled toward the fallen tree where he intended to build his fire. Twice he stopped, but only to gather a few small branches.

When he reached the far right of the clearing, the sun was pasted behind the trees and cast long shadows into the clearing and partway up the cliff face. The rock burned orange between the spidery tendrils of shadow.

He deposited the branches at the fallen tree, then crawled into the clearing to retrieve others. When he had gathered what he could from the clearing, he turned his attention to the woods. He knew the fallen tree itself had branches that he could hack away, but he feared there were too few to last the night.

He gathered what he judged to be enough wood to burn many hours, as well as some papery birch bark, which he stuffed into his vest pocket. The pain in his leg whined with a hot, unbroken intensity, and his hands were red and stiff with cold. His fingers felt as if they would shatter if he struck them against the ground.

At least the wood was dry. It had been a dry winter. Maybe the driest he had ever experienced. Before today, there had been four straight days of thaw. There was no snow. Still, it was below freezing now, and he knew the cold would deepen when the sun vanished behind the mountains.

For awhile, he rested near the tree, his back against the rock wall, and tried to warm his hands by sliding them beneath his vest and under his armpits. Their coldness chilled him even through his shirt. The sun was balanced like a saucer on the rim of the mountains, and he watched it through his smoking breath.

If this had to happen, why couldn't it be summer? Then he'd have heat. Heat was normally something you took for granted. Now, suddenly, it was monumental. Imagine your life depending on something as inconsequential as a flame. But he could see it was true. A man had to take care of the little things in life before he could turn his attention to anything of consequence. How many other things had he taken for granted? They could kill him now.

He slid his hands out and looked at them. They were still red, and they were stiff and numb when he flexed his fingers. He moved his hands to the shirt button on his breast and tried to unbutton it so he could slide his hands against his skin. But he could not make his fingers work. He watched them fumble at the button like two clusters of insentient sticks. He tried pushing the button through the buttonhole while he pulled on the pocket flap and, finally, he worked the button through. Quickly, he pulled his shirt open and clamped his hands beneath his arms. Their coldness cut deep. It was worse than the cold of the compass when he first dropped it inside his shirt. He moved one hand. The compass was there, lying flat on his chest.

Then he waited and watched the red sun sink until its rim winked above the silhouetted mountains and then was gone altogether.

There was less than an hour of twilight left, and then his world would be utterly black.

As he watched the glow of amethyst and orange along the mountaintops, his shivering sank away from his skin and began to shake deep within him. He held himself and tried not to think.

"Damn this cold." He shouldn't wait any longer. He could wait himself into a grave. No, no. He needed to take time. Try to get his hands back.

He waited another quarter of an hour before he drew his hands out and beat them against his legs to force some circulation. The pain sliced his fingers like a knife. He flexed his fingers against the pain before he removed the birch bark from his pocket and shredded it clumsily and placed it on the ground under the tree trunk. Then he set to breaking and arranging kindling over the scraps of bark. He could feel the cold wood stealing more of the feeling from his fingers.

There was only the shaky sound of his breathing now and, in between the intervals of silence, the dry snap of the kindling. The birds and other creatures had gone silent. The sun had long disappeared, with just the palest glow stretching along the dark mountains and fading from the blackening sky. The first stars were visible.

In the growing darkness, the kindling became a mound with less and less detail, and he knew when the night was total he might not be able to see the wood at all.

When he had laid enough kindling to hold a fire, he tried to unbutton his shirt pocket, but his fingers burned with cold and were nearly dead.

He let out a deep, shaking breath, and felt his frustration tighten.

"Pull the damn button off if you have to, but get those fucking matches."

With one hand pressed against the bottom of the pocket, he slipped two fingers under the pocket's flap and pulled hard. He heard tearing and then his hand shot free. His fingers felt as if they had been slashed, and he yelped and thrust his hand under his arm.

Keep it there. Let it warm so you can use it. So he waited and watched the darkness deepen, but his fingers did not revive. He could feel them stealing the warmth from his body.

He couldn't wait any longer.

With his left hand pressed against the bottom of his shirt pocket, he used his right fist to nudge upward the rawhide pouch he sought. He tried to close his fingers on its lace, but he could not tell whether he actually held the lace. He lifted his hand and his arm felt weight. But the pouch slipped and fell against his leg.

Damn. He hadn't thought it through. He should have taken the matches out hours ago. Wasn't this just what his old man would expect?

A spasm shook him, and his heart felt like it was shivering against his ribs.

He had to keep his head. He had to concentrate on the matches and not let the fear get the better of him.

Again he slipped his hands inside his shirt against his skin. Then he leaned forward and waited. While he waited, the darkness deepened until it was complete.

It was time enough. It might be more than time enough.

He went back to work quickly, this time scooping the pouch into his hands. He raised it and worked the lace into his mouth and unwound it and dumped the pouch's contents between his legs.

With the claw of his right hand, he pushed the pile flat and located the metal can of matches with his wrist, but when he could not pick the can up, he pried his left hand open on the ground and rolled the can into it with the cupped fingers of the other. Then he pressed his hands over the can and raised it and clamped it between his teeth. With his tongue, he confirmed the lid was in his mouth. There was a metallic run in his saliva. Then he bit on the can and pulled. The can jerked forward, cutting his lower lip, and he tasted blood, bitter and metallic. He drew the can back and pulled again.

There was no give.

He increased the pressure of his hands and pulled harder. His hands suddenly shot away. He started and tried to pull them back, but too late. He heard the can hit the ground somewhere out in the darkness.

He sat utterly still. For a moment, he did not even shiver. Then he spat out the lid and stared after it, but the darkness was so complete, even his boots a few feet away, were nearly invisible.

"Oh my god."

In an instant, he circled his legs behind and dropped onto his stomach. The pain ripped at his leg.

He crawled forward, groping in the darkness, but, except for pain, his fingers could not feel. On he crawled, running his arms over the ground to his right and left. He felt many rocks, but not the can. Where was it? It had to be out there.

He crawled on.

Nothing.

Then some more.

Nothing.

He rested his forehead against the cold leaves.

How in hell was he going to a light match even if he found the can? His hands didn't work.

His insides were jittery, and he quaked once, deep and hard. His leg was burning like acetylene.

What was the use? If luck was against you, you couldn't win. He wiped his eyes with the back of his hand. He should've just stayed where he fell and let the cold take him. Maybe then they wouldn't know. Maybe all they could say when they found him would be: Poor bastard. What do you suppose made him fall?

He pounded the ground with the heel of his palm. "Damn."

And then it occurred to him. If his fingers could not feel, his palms still could. He could hold a match between his palms.

Quickly, he was up on his forearms, dragging himself forward, checking the ground to either side of him.

He found nothing.

He moved forward a few inches. He did it again and again until the fear went in and out of him fast on his breathing.

It had to be out there!

He went forward one more time. Then he thought he saw it—a

small, compact object a few inches from his face, barely visible in the starlight.

He moved his arm forward and touched it with his wrist, and he felt a sudden burst of warmth. But when he tried to pick up the can, he could not will his fingers to work. He could not even tell whether the can was empty or full.

The shivering came back, quaking, and his hands shook. He brought his head down and probed the can with his tongue. There were matches inside, but only a few. He moved his face along the ground a few feet to the right, and he thought he felt them. With his tongue, he touched the tiny shafts on the leaves. Then he bit and pulled the matches and leaves away. He circled and dragged himself back toward the fallen tree. The tree and the tepee of kindling materialized out of the darkness only when he was inches from them.

He pressed his hands over the wad and placed it in his lap and spat out the musty residue and licked the cut in his lip.

He tried to find a match with his fingers once, twice, three times. No use. There was still feeling in his palms, and after many minutes, he was able to roll a match between his hands.

It took a long time to work the tip outward, and he could not distinguish whether it was the flammable end that was extended. He found a rock with his elbow and struck out with the match.

The match flared and settled, and for a moment the tepee of wood assumed detail, but then the flame lapped at his hands. He dropped the match and watched the flame on the leaves as it receded, turned blue, then went black.

He was in too much of a hurry. He had matches now and he could light them. He ought to warm his hands.

He burrowed his hands inside his shirt and shuddered, then stiffened. Then he waited, feeling the cold deepen now that night was absolute.

In his mind he saw himself, a stiff, ashen-skinned figure, frozen and sitting upright, his eyes glazed with ice, staring into the yawning solitude.

He shook off the image, but it left him tingling.

Maybe he shouldn't wait. Maybe his mind was starting to go.

No-no-no-no-no. He had to wait.

But what if his hands were gone for good? Look how he was shivering. That was how it started. He remembered how it was with Dick.

He withdrew his hands and pressed the wad of leaves between them and felt for a match with his nose. With his teeth, he pulled the match out, then replaced the leaves in his lap. Again, he worked the match between his hands. Then he struck at the rock.

The match flared, hissing. This time the flame was out from his hands, but the flame withdrew quickly into a puny glow.

"Tip it down, you idiot!" He turned his hands slightly.

The flame brightened, but wavered.

"Please, for god's sake, hands."

He moved the flame to the wood and concentrated on steadying his hands.

At first there was nothing, just the feeble glow of the match. But then the light swelled, and he smelled smoke. He held onto the match even when the flame licked his skin; he held on until he could feel the first breath of heat on his face. Then he dropped the match and, sucking his hand, held his breath.

"Please, for the love of god."

He could hear his heart in his ears before he could hear another sound—the hushed, but rising, breath of the fire.

He released his own breath then, and everything inside seemed to cave in.

Sweet Jesus. It was going to burn!

July 1916

It was nearly a year since his aunt brought him to her white colonial in Bennington. In all that time, he seldom left his room on the second floor. The memory of what he did to his father seemed less real if he kept himself shut away, especially from the woods. And there was Emma, too, his aunt who looked so much like his mother that it sometimes pained him to look at her.

He spent his days at the window, looking at the mountains, at Harmon Hill. He watched how the mountains transformed with the seasons: burning with oranges and reds and yellows in the autumn sunlight beneath skies of brilliant blue; brittle with browns and blues and purples in winter, stark against dark, tattered clouds; and, finally, green and fulsome in spring, but fading, wilting with summer to the way they looked the day his aunt brought him there. He had seen it all before, around their farm in upstate Vermont. But he felt no desire to go into this wilderness that surrounded his present just as that other wilderness, his father's, had surrounded his past. He was untouchable by the woods—by his father—as long as he stayed in his room.

When he was not watching the mountains, he read. His

Uncle Eric (who had actually graduated from college) had stocked a library on the first floor. When his aunt and uncle were away from the house, he tiptoed down the stairs and into the library. The walls were lined with white bookcases, which were filled with books, many of them leather bound. He loved to run his fingers over the bindings when he selected books. Shakespeare's *Macbeth* was bound in red, Twain's *Adventures of Tom Sawyer* in green. When he had a half dozen books, he tiptoed back up the stairs and returned to his room, not to be seen again until summoned for meals, and even then only for the time required to consume sparse helpings of meat and vegetables.

But Emma and Eric seemed to understand. "Don't hurry it," he overheard the doctor tell them. "Be patient. In time he'll come out of it. Horrible, to have lost both parents while still so young. To have seen his father die like that. Horrible shock; but it will pass."

But his need for solitude did not pass, not until Carrie appeared in the yard next door.

It was late June. He heard a voice through the open window and put his book aside. She was playing with Nathan and Elizabeth, the toddler children next door.

She appeared to be about his age, not more than eighteen anyway. She had brown hair and was slender. There seemed nothing remarkable about her, just her hands, for she had long fingers. Much longer than his aunt's. And she was pretty. Was that how he would describe her?

Perhaps. But if merely pretty, certainly not ordinary. For he could not keep himself from looking at her. Was it because of her awkward way with the children, how she seemed both to enjoy them and their games and, at the same time, not quite know what to do with them? That was the way he would be, too, he thought.

But, no. It was more. She was like a beacon, as if all light were condensed in her and then radiated from her. He was powerless to pull his eyes away, and he was filled with the strangest feeling as he looked at her, at her soft brown hair and radiant face. He felt a longing, a hungry emptiness that seemed to feed on her radiating light, yet was not satisfied.

All of July, he watched her unseen, studied how she moved, tried to anticipate how she would wear her hair (either pinned in a bun at the back of her head, or simply pulled back and tied behind so that it fell between her shoulders), delighted in how she seemed to float when she walked, to drift, as if her slender body, her long skirt, were a ship moving effortlessly through a sea of grass. And then there was how she laughed. Her laughter was full of sunlight. He could think of no other way to describe it. It was like the distillation of summer itself, warm and alive, and each time he saw her he longed to hear her laugh, dreamed that someday he might be a catalyst for that laughter.

One day, he watched and listened as she played pattacake with Elizabeth.

"Patticake, patticake, baker's man.

Bake me a cake as fast as you can.

Roll it, and pat it, and mark it with a 'B,'

and throw it in the oven for baby and me."

She said it with a sweet, lilting voice, and Elizabeth squealed with laughter with the 'B' that was traced on her tummy. "Again!" she shouted.

But that was not how the rhyme went. He knew because it was the one his mother had recited over and over to him, and this new way wasn't correct.

He rushed from his room, descended the stairs two at a time, and turned up the hallway, through the kitchen, not even stopping at his aunt's startled: "My god, David. You've left your room!" Out the back door he went, across the yard and up to the picket fence that separated their houses.

31

"That's not how it goes!" he insisted.

Startled, she looked up and stood and eyed him, nudging Elizabeth behind her.

And then, softer: "I mean—that's not how it goes."

"How then?" she said.

His resolve wilted under her eyes. He tried to calm himself by grasping the tops of the pickets.

"It's Pattacake, pattacake, baker's man.

Bake me a cake as fast as you can.

Pat it, and prick it, and mark it with a 'B,'

And put it in the oven for baby and me."

She seemed neither startled nor perplexed. She was a blank—serene, inscrutable, radiant. He felt silly, obscenely conspicuous. And he could feel his face coloring. But when he looked at her, she smiled, and just as he dropped his eyes, she said pleasantly, with a little laugh and tone of delighted surprise: "I'm Carrie. And please tell, who are you?"

"I know," he said. "I've known it from the day I first saw you."

3

He placed more wood on his fire. In awhile, the flames burned upward and outward and lapped against the fallen tree and into the night with the breathless rustling of tiny flags.

He sat close to the fire, his legs out straight, parallel to the tree, his hands held near the flames. The pain boiled in his fingers as the heat ate inward, and he hardly gave his leg any mind.

"Sweet jesus," he said, sucking breath. It felt like someone was peeling the flesh off down to the bones.

He shouldn't bellyache, he supposed. He'd come damn close to buying it, and he ought to be tickled he was feeling anything. He just had to wait now. In another hour or so the pain in his hands would be behind him and then he could worry about tomorrow.

He lifted a piece of wood between clamped hands and leaned it on the fire, then watched the flames lick into the night. He knew the sky was broken only by the pinholes of stars, but because of the fire, he could not see the stars. Except for a breathing light that extended several yards in a circle, the world was vacant and black.

"Tomorrow." He said the word softly and looked into the fire.

Tomorrow? He snorted. It didn't take a genius to figure this out. The bitch of it was, why did he feel like he'd been had? Life was so damn amusing. He spent most of his believing that he didn't have anything to live for, especially after Carrie. But now... Now living seemed an important thing. The only thing. How was it that you could go through life and not realize something until it was too late?

What else was there? He didn't want to go out full of regret.

It was something to think about, though, wasn't it? Your own death. He supposed everyone thought about it once in awhile. Yet, even now, with death maybe a day or two away if he was unlucky, he still couldn't picture how it would come, what it would be like. But the thought of it frightened him.

He remembered finding a sprung trap once, with the chewed-off paw of a raccoon in its teeth. He figured that raccoon must have known it was going to die. But it was better not giving into it. It was better to go out on your own terms.

He wouldn't give into it, either. He couldn't—not any more than that raccoon could. You couldn't go against your nature. If he'd learned anything, he'd learned that. He just didn't want to be full of regret.

He churned the coals with a stick and looked into the leaping flames. Then he drew a deep breath and let it out in a rush that made the embers brighten an instant.

Well, it wouldn't be tonight. If he didn't make any mistakes, he might even hold out for a few days. Who knew? Maybe Dick would come. You could never count luck out altogether.

He looked at his hands and flexed them and held them to the fire again. His damp clothes were steaming into the night air.

He stayed close to the fire until his clothes were dry and the pain was gone from his fingers. Then he moved back against the wall of rock. The smokiness of the fire was in his clothes, and it was pleasant to be warm again and to feel the heat around him.

He was just a kid when his old man taught him to sit like that, with his body between the fire and rock. 'That way the fire warms your front, and the heat reflecting off the rock helps to toast your backside. A greenhorn's the only one that builds a fire between hisself and rock.'

It had to be twenty-five years now. It was like all the things his old man taught him about the woods. They were part of him, in the same way as the brown of his hair or the green of his eyes. Without his choosing. But then, you never did have a choice with his old man. You did what he expected, and you did it one way, his way. And that meant you did it absolutely perfect, or you did it again.

He couldn't help wonder, though: if his mother had lived, how would he have turned out? If she lived, his old man wouldn't have had a reason for all the torment he'd put him through.

It was then that he felt it—the sensation that something was watching him.

He scanned the darkness beyond the fire. But there was

nothing—no sound, nothing to look at except darkness. He was alone. And yet, as he often did in the woods at night, he felt the presence of some other living thing, something concealed and watching him. It was different from what he had sensed that day when he was five; there wasn't any fear in it now. Did the wilderness have a soul? A consciousness? Some essence that had persisted for eons? Maybe it was just the fire that made him feel this way. It blotted the world into darkness while illuminating him for all the world to see.

Sometimes he believed it was his old man watching him, and that scared him a little because if there was anyone who could come back to finish his business, it was his old man.

He peered into the blackness. "No, old Jacob," he said softly, "I didn't do what I was supposed to that day. I didn't die. And it tormented you up until the very end."

That day was the only one in his life that he enjoyed letting his old man down. Hah, by succeeding, of all things. But there was no sense that he prevailed. He merely endured, survived.

He sighed.

Maybe this was his time to prevail. When the odds were stacked against him.

He churned the coals.

Well, he wasn't dead yet, and he was intent on disappointing his old man one more time. He'd give anything to do it. Sometimes that seemed what his early years boiled down to. Letting his old man down. By not doing things right. When was the first?

His first time hunting maybe? No, the first time had to be before that. He could remember that time well enough, though...

He was nine. Old enough to use a gun. That's what his old man said. That summer, out in the pasture, he showed him how to shoot, how to steady the gun and sight along the barrel. He could be patient with things like that, with the showing.

But he couldn't steady the gun. He was too small, and the gun was too big, taller than he was, and heavy. His old man didn't want to hear any of that, though. He said he was ready, and that was that. Just keep practicing.

He didn't want to do it; that was the rest of it. He didn't think he could. He thought about it all the time when they were scouting the buck. For two days they scouted it. Not hunting. Not then. Just learning its habits—where it foraged, where it bedded, when it moved, and where, until his old man knew what that buck was going to do even before the buck realized it.

Then they did hunt it. It was December. And it was cold. Jesus, it was cold. It was still hours before dawn when they started out. They went across the field behind the house, past his mother's grave, and he remembered how pale her gravestone was in the moonlight and how quiet it was walking out in the night so cold it felt like iron. There was only the sound of their feet in the grass, the grass dry and brittle, white with hoar and sparkling in the moonlight. And as he went past her grave, he couldn't help remembering how she looked the day she died, watching them load her into the wagon. And he could remember thinking, praying: 'Mother, please stop him; don't let Pa make me,' or something like that, because he just couldn't understand how his old man expected him to do that again to another living thing, even a deer. But his old man noticed him lagging, as if he knew what was going through his mind. 'Come on,' he said. 'Pick it up. Pick it up.'

So on they went, and he kept his mouth shut.

Then they were at the end of the field where the woods started, the moon ghostly and bright through the tree branches as they went into it. A hunter's moon. He could remember the weight of the gun at that moment, and he could see the gun, too, black and cold in the moonlight. It might have been easier if only he didn't have to look at it, but the moon was so big, and he kept picturing the end of the rifle spitting fire, but by then they were in the woods, and there was no talking. That was the rule. No talking once they reached the woods. 'Talking should've been done long before we got here.' Another one of the famous rules. So he kept quiet. There was just the sound of his own feet shushing on the leaves as they moved into it, but not his old man's. No. He moved like he wasn't a man, but something already dead, a tall dark shape in the moonlight, a shadow that moved without noise.

They didn't go to where the buck bedded, but to a trail it used for watering. 'Comes this way 'most every day,' his old man said while they were scouting it.

He took out the bottle of fox urine then and soaked a rag with it, then followed the trail, the rag on a string, skipping on the ground to cover their smell, to make the buck curious.

They must have been still far from the stream because he

couldn't remember hearing it when his old man tapped him and pointed for him to hide in a blow-down. The buck would walk right up to them he told him, because of the urine.

It was to be his shot. And he was thinking about that as he climbed into the branches and set himself. He went over it in his mind: his old man would tap him when it was time to shoot. No shooting until he tapped. That was the rule. Don't waste a shot. Worse, don't miss a vital spot. Wounding was worse than missing. Don't make an animal suffer. A hunter's worse offense, and he wouldn't abide it.

Then they waited in the still, rigid cold and watched the moon set and the blackness grow gray and dim. He remembered how he couldn't stop shivering, waiting there, clutching the rifle that was too big, too heavy, that he knew he would not be able to steady. Feeling his fingers go numb on the stock. Worrying that he wouldn't have the nerve, or that he wouldn't be able to hit it behind the shoulder, through the fourth rib, like his old man had told him. Through the hours of waiting, he thought about killing it, about actually seeing the living, breathing animal at the end of the barrel and then squeezing the trigger. But that's where it stopped. He couldn't imagine beyond the squeezing, what it would look like, whether it would make any sound. And there was his old man to wonder about, too. What he would do if he couldn't shoot. It just went on and on, and all the time the shivering kept getting worse.

And then it happened. His old man nudged him. But when he looked, he didn't see anything and, for a moment, he thought maybe he was signaling him to head back, maybe they had waited long enough. But then he saw the buck, too, so big, the head with the big rack of spreading antlers. The shivering was right around his heart as he watched the buck come on, slowly, walking out of the dim light of dawn, following the scent, just like a dog, just like his old man said it would. Walking, stopping, lowering its head to smell, walking again.

He wanted to yell to it, to warn it before it was too late. It was so close he could see the muscles of its chest even in the dim light. But it was too late. His old man tapped him and it started.

He struggled to raise the gun, feeling it waver from the shivering and the waiting and the weight. So heavy. Bringing it up but not able to steady it, hearing it click against a branch.

The buck stopped, just an instant, then sprang toward the trees.

'Shoot!' his old man said under his breath, whistling loud before he had hardly finished saying it. The buck stopped dead and turned its head toward them. It was all happening so fast, unfolding before he could even think or knew how to react.

'Shoot, damn it!' his old man said again. And then he heard the explosion, the roar and recoil of the gun kicking him over backwards, but he had been able to look long enough. The buck was going down, too, so he knew he'd hit it. He'd hit it!

That's why he couldn't believe it when he got up. The buck was gone. He wasn't quite to his feet when his old man hauled back and hit him backhanded across the face, so hard, he went down again, backwards, into the branches of the blow-down.

'Damn you! You hit him in the ass! A goddamn hind shot, you son of a bitch. I'll have to track him now. Get out of my sight before I give you more than that. Go on, get out of here. Go home!'

He didn't try to get up. He crawled along the ground dragging the rifle with him, looking up at the utter disgust in his old man's eyes as he struggled to get out of the branches. Then he was free, and he had the gun free, too, and he ran. He didn't cry, not until he was far away. And then he slowed to a walk, and it came out of him, not because of what his old man had done, but because of the buck. He'd missed… in the worst possible way. He thought about the bleeding and the pain the buck was suffering. He wanted to believe that the buck would be okay if only his old man didn't find it. But he knew that was a lie, just like he knew his old man would find it and would shoot it, that he'd stay out no matter how long it took because you didn't put an animal through that.

It was still morning when he reached the house. He waited by the window all that morning. All afternoon, too. Thinking about what he'd done. And he thought about his old man out there stalking it, wondering what he'd do when he got home.

Even after the sun had gone down, he was still by the window. And then he saw his old man suddenly walk out of the night, the gutted buck slung over his shoulders, not looking like a deer anymore, but like some awful imitation in the light from the window — stiff, wooden, the tongue lolling from its mouth.

He ran from the window, retreating behind the stuffed armchair, and heard the carcass thud onto the porch. Then his old man came in. He closed the door quietly and leaned his back against it a moment without looking at him.

He studied his old man's face, but all he could see was the tiredness, like he was the one that had been stalked all day and shot. He didn't speak to him, but after a while he stood away from the door and, slowly, started toward him. He could remember how fast his heart was going, thinking, here it comes; he'll beat me now, but when his old man put his arm out, it was just to grab the chair, and then he slumped into it and shut his eyes.

He moved away from the chair, out of reach, and watched him sitting there with his eyes closed. The smell of the buck was on him, its blood, too, dark and drying deep in the fibers of his jacket. So it seemed almost like it was the still-suffering buck he was watching, the buck that, at any moment, would open its eyes and curse him for what he had done, what it was enduring.

His old man's eyes did open then. They looked like they did on those nights when he sat in front of the fire, just staring, the look he sometimes had when Aunt Emma was around. Tired, but more than that he realized now, with some kind of terrible hurt lurking behind the tiredness.

The silence was so deep and long that it actually startled him when his old man did speak, looking at him only a second.

'Suppose there wasn't no need hitting you like that.' He closed his eyes. 'But I ain't sorry for it. And you'll remember that, I reckon. And you'll remember that it wasn't nothing compared to what you done to that buck.'

Then he was quiet again. His old man opened his eyes and looked at him a long time. He could feel the eyes moving over his face, always moving, but never off of him.

He looked back, and there was everything in his old man's eyes, all the pain and hardship that both creatures had suffered, but that only one had survived.

But what in god's name did he want from him? What was he supposed to say? That he was sorry? Oh, god, he was sorry, sorry that he pulled the trigger at all. But his old man must have known what was going through his mind.

'Save it,' he said without emotion. 'There ain't nothing you can say now that can set it right. Just go to bed.'

He stirred the embers and, with the stick, tried to reposition the wood to burn hotter, but suddenly he stopped and looked long and deep into the flames before he let his eyes close.

No, there was never any enjoyment out of letting his old man down. Only that one time.

He looked up toward the stars, and he could picture how they would look—cold, almost crystalline, so distant and silent in the depthless blanket of night.

He didn't want to die. Good god, he didn't want to. Not yet. There had to be some way to stop it.

The first thrusts of anguish surged within him. But he tightened himself and clenched his teeth and fought against it, and, in awhile, he was calm again. But he felt an emptiness, a loneliness, within him as measureless as the night sky that sprawled above and that a million stars could not fill or light, and his mind kept on going back to the day he had walked out of the woods on his father.

It had changed him forever, that day. The wilderness, too, he realized now. Or at least how he perceived it. He supposed it was impossible not to feel that he'd been made a fool of for seven years. After that, it was like he had to prove something. What? That he was better than the wilderness? That he could beat it?

That's what had brought him to this. And he knew now that all of it had had to wait for this day.

Another of his great discoveries!

Yet it was true, wasn't it? If he was going to beat it, it would have to be on its terms. That last time, he had endured, he had survived, but he had not prevailed.

Well, he didn't like the terms much this time, but they were set and he would have to live with them... Or die with them.

He wriggled his fingers before the flames.

That was more like it. In a little while, they'd be as good as new and he'd have time to think. A man ought to be able to come out on top of something that couldn't think. It ought to make a difference. But he knew it didn't.

Then he remembered: the match can. He needed to retrieve it.

It was amazing what a man could forget with a little too much comfort, even something that had given him back his life.

He crawled away from the fire, and the cold air pressed around him. First he retrieved the can and then picked up the matches he could find and placed them in the can. He'd look for others in the daylight, he told himself as he moved toward the fire. He marveled how cold the air felt, as if he had crawled into an icehouse out of blazing summer heat. At the fire, he tilted the can to the firelight and counted. About two dozen, he figured. Maybe not enough if they had to last five or six days.

He replaced the lid just tight enough to keep moisture out, then returned the can to his shirt pocket.

He settled himself and, when he was satisfied that the fire was burning well, he inspected the items from the pouch—a metal mirror; a whistle on a leather lanyard; a small magnifying lens. At least a dozen cracks radiated from the center of the lens.

It was too bad about that. The lens might have saved some matches if there was sunshine during the next day or two. But, there were other ways to make a lens. His old man once showed him how to make a lens from ice. He tossed the lens into the fire.

He returned the other items to the pouch and wound the lace two times around its leather button.

"You see that, pack!" he shouted into the night. "You did not get everything. I have fooled you a little, too." He lifted the pouch over his head and jiggled it, then put the pouch into his shirt pocket.

Who was he kidding? The matches were the only thing he'd need. There wouldn't be anyone to signal. But a woodsman stacked the odds in his favor beforehand. Right, old Jacob?

He looked at his leg.

"Well, leg. What do you say?"

He cocked his head.

"No, not far. Just a few trips along the base here. See for yourself. We haven't gathered wood enough for the night, else I wouldn't ask you."

Jesus, he was getting soft. Well, what harm was there in talking to his leg... as long as he didn't hear it talk back.

He dropped onto his side and crawled to the other side of the clearing. Away from the fire, he could see the stars, and they looked as he had imagined—rigid, silent, crystalline. Altogether, he chopped and dragged back four branches, plus a long forked branch. From this he could fashion a crutch, he told himself. He inspected the branch in the firelight.

He'd make better time if he didn't have to crawl everywhere. He only wished there was a way to get on that ledge and get his coat and pack. Well, he'd just have to travel a few hours at a stretch. When he got cold, he would light a fire. If he could do a mile a day, he'd be out of this in two days. At worst, three. The matches ought to last that long, if he was careful.

That was the way to think. He'd beaten all of the bad luck so far, hadn't he? Wait and see, by morning there would be a little numbness in his leg, and then, who knew?

He grabbed the branch and leaned against the rock and let his eyes follow the smoke skyward. He pictured the moon rising even though he knew the full moon was still two weeks away. No, there would be only the stars, numberless as the invisible trees and glowing too weakly to light the darkness.

He took his knife from its sheath and, positioning the forked branch against the rocks, broke the tines to size. Then he laid his body flat, and pushed the fork under his armpit, and scuffed the ground with his heel. He eased his shoulder from the tines and sat up, being careful not to move the branch and, with his knife, scarred the limb a few inches below the scuff mark. Then he moved back against the cliff face and began to whittle at the scar. He thought about using the hatchet. It would be faster. But then, finding another branch like this might not be easy, and he could not risk a misaimed blow. He couldn't afford to take any risks now or make any more mistakes.

If he got out of this, he could just picture telling Dick, his eyes getting all big the way they did. Dick respected anyone who could get on in the wilderness. Falling from the ledge wouldn't matter any. 'Hell,' he'd say, 'that kind of thing can happen to anyone. I'm so clumsy, I've been known to trip over dust in my cabin.' Sad thing was, that was true.

He stopped whittling and chuckled. Then he shook his head and was at it again.

It was too bad Dick never knew his old man. In the woods, he was sure something. He'd have to give the bastard that. He thought of him like he thought of the Indians, though his old man always denied it. 'It ain't the same,' he told him once. 'I'm a farmer, boy, and a woodsman only part time. But the Indians... They was part of the woods, like a leaf is part of a tree. Hell, they was the woods.'

It didn't matter; he always thought about his old man in just those terms: hell, he was the woods.

Old Jacob expected as much from him, but he hadn't taught him how. He knew now it wasn't something you could teach. It was the one thing that made his old man different from any other man he ever knew.

He broke the limb at the whittled spot, then rested it on the ground with the point above the coals for the heat to make it hard.

The wood he had gathered was plentiful. Still, it would not last the night he feared. He crawled to the end of the fallen tree and, pulling himself onto his good leg, hacked at the tree's branches with his hatchet. Every once in awhile, he returned to the fire and pulled out the crutch to let it cool, then put it near the coals again.

When he had finished chopping, he rested and let his eyes rise with the smoke. The smoke was white against the blackness. Beyond the smoke, he could picture Orion and the other constellations wheeling in the silence of the frigid darkness.

He wished he was like the smoke. He wished he could just rise up and drift out of this. Even the animals had it easier. A man had to take what he needed; he had to think. All the hard thinking, all the learning, had been behind him, and now he was back to it. Only it didn't feel right. It didn't feel natural.

He wished he had a full moon. The Algonquin had called this the month of the Snow Moon because the heaviest snows fell during February. They also called it the month of the Hunger Moon because the snows made hunting difficult. Either was so much better than February. There was something of themselves in names like those. What the hell was February to anyone?

Maybe if he was an Indian he'd have a better idea of how to get out of this. Time would tell. Time was the one thing that always told the truth. The time for the Indians was passed, and now it was his time.

He went down on one elbow and pulled the crutch from the fire for the last time and dropped another branch into the flames. A shower of sparks raced skyward through the smoke and went black against the inky vault of night. Then he laid on the ground, close to the bed of coals, and looked up, and he felt the tiredness weighing heavy within him, more tiredness than he could ever remember, even on those nights after he had logged from sunup to sundown.

In a little while, he was asleep. In his dreaming, he saw the Indians. They were suddenly there, without his having heard them, as if they had risen out of the very earth. Their eyes were dark and clear, fierce eyes that could look at any man's and not flinch. They were unlike any man's eyes he had ever seen. The Indians seemed stronger than other men, too, with a wildness that was strange to him, so they assumed great stature in his dreaming.

They gathered around him, muttering in a tongue he did not understand, and they pointed at his leg and looked him in the eye as they spoke. But there was one who did not speak. He stood away from the others, and he fixed him with eyes that never blinked, never moved, until the talking stopped.

Then he came forward and he knelt and he placed one hand on his shoulder and gripped him hard. And he knew then that they considered him worthy. They could see from the signs in the clearing that he had suffered much. They could see from his leg that he was no coward and was not afraid of pain. And they could see from the piled wood and the fire that he was no quitter. He could tell all of that from the way the hand gripped his shoulder.

Then he woke because he was chilled. It was only long enough to feed the fire. He wanted to return to his dream of the Indians.

But in his second dream, he could not make them come back. The clearing was empty, and the wilderness around him was empty, too.

"All gone."

He dreamt the words, and the wilderness rang with the sound of them, somber, carried on a moaning wind. And the words sounded sad in his dreaming, ringing as they did in the solitude. And he felt sorry that the Indians were all gone… all dead.

March 1920

There was already reason enough to fear Sykes, for Sykes had a foul disposition that projected itself through a face so angular and taut, it appeared to be fixed in a perpetual snarl. That face glowered from atop a bull's frame, and all of it, face and body alike, looking for all the world to be covered, not by skin, but by some queer conglomeration of leather patches sewn together and toughened from too long exposure to the elements.

Sykes had labored more than twenty years as a logger, and his physical attributes were the sum total of that existence, except his eyes. Sykes had the coldest eyes he had ever seen. They were not so much mean as they were devoid of any human caring—two ice-blue stones set deep in the face of some hideous leather doll. And that face gave to Sykes the impression that he could chew through a saddle, not only without difficulty, but perhaps with actual pleasure. And there was indication that he might have attempted that feat, for Sykes was missing one canine tooth, which gave to his smile a disquieting malevolence. Some said he lost the tooth in a bar fight, not from any punch, but from biting another man's forearm so savagely four men had to pry him free. Even then, Sykes had never loosened his hold, or so the story went, and when Sykes was finally pulled off, the tooth had stayed behind, imbedded in the other man's mutilated arm.

So there was already reason enough to fear Sykes. But now there was another: after four weeks in camp, it was clear that Sykes hated him. He could not plumb the reason for the hatred, but, clearly, Sykes hated him, with a passion that seemed as all consuming as it was mindless. Almost from the moment he set foot in camp, Sykes took a dislike to him. Maybe it was because he kept to himself, or because he was bookish. Or maybe it was because he would not participate in the drinking and whoring in Montreal which was the loggers' Saturday night pastime. Instead, he remained at camp—alone, reading. Even if the pain of Carrie was far behind him, he would not join the men in their carnal pursuit. Maybe that was where the hatred started. But in four weeks, another thing was obvious to everyone in camp, including Sykes—that at twenty, not much more than a boy—he was a far better woodsman than Sykes and knew more about the woods than the other would ever know. And that embittered Sykes the more.

But today there was a more immediate reason for fear.

It was Saturday, just after noon. He was lying on the top bunk, reading. It was not his bunk, but the bunk was near a window, where the light was better, and Tug Iverson, whose bunk it was, said it was okay. Sykes started on him as he had several times during the past two weeks, not talking to him, but about him, in an over-loud voice for all the others, who were grooming themselves for the evening, to hear. But this time it was different because Sykes was drinking, was, in fact, already drunk on Sutter's moonshine. Yet it was not Sykes's words that made him nervous as much as the menace in his voice.

"Hey, boys," Sykes roared, "am I seeing things, or does he move his lips when he reads?" He laughed oafishly.

He did not take his eyes from the page, though he stopped seeing the words and was mindful of Sykes's whereabouts.

"How 'bout reading out loud for me and the boys? Com'on, smart boy. Read out loud to us."

He kept his eyes fixed on the page.

Then he heard Sykes start for the bunk, his boots hitting the floor in a hard, jerky cadence, the incoherent choreography of alcohol. The stench of his breath arrived before the man.

Sykes wavered by the side of the bunk. His hair was cropped short, so short, it gave the appearance that one could sand lumber by rubbing it against his head. Sykes's gray shirt was stretched tight over his muscular frame.

"Hey, you. Boy," Sykes said, putting his hand over the book. "You hear me talking to you?"

"What?"

"I said I'm talking to you. You answer when I talk, you hear me? What kind of garbage you reading there anyway?"

He showed Sykes the cover. *Adventures of Huckleberry Finn.*

"Answer me, goddamn it! When I ask a question, you answer. You can talk, can't you?"

"Yes."

"Yes what?"

"Yes. I can talk."

"Well, you talk then when I'm speaking to you. Don't go shoving no fucking book in my face."

"I didn't... I was—"

"—Don't go telling me you didn't. You calling me a liar, you fucking fairy?"

"Jerry, leave him alone," one of the men said. "He's a

good kid. Leave him be."

"Up yours," Sykes snapped, turning back and smacking the book out of his hands. It shot along the floor across the room "I asked if you was calling me a liar."

He shook his head no.

"Speak, goddamn it! You speak to me when I'm talking to you." Sykes grabbed him by his shirtfront then and pulled him from the bunk, spilling him hard onto the plank floor. "Get up."

He stood up slowly. Sykes was not a tall man, but he was so muscled and compact, he gave the impression of enormous power.

"Go 'head," Sykes said to him. "You take the first poke. Make it a good one, though. I don't intend to let you get another."

"Look, Jerry, I'm—"

"—I said take a poke," Sykes roared.

He shook his head no.

Sykes pushed him then, one powerful thrust. "Swing on me, I said." He could hear Sykes's hatred seething in and out on his breath.

"No. I'm not looking for any trouble," he replied, mindful to keep his tone cool, unemotional. Then he walked away, but when he bent to pick up his book, a ferocious kick to the buttocks propelled him head first into the wood piled by the potbelly stove. The logs clattered to the floor. Some of the men laughed.

Then Sykes was over him again, wavering. "Get up and fight," he growled, his breath fouling the air.

He looked at Sykes from the floor and shook his head. "No. I won't fight you."

"Either you get up, faggot, or I'll beat you where you sit. You know, I'm thinking that's exactly what your problem is. Been wondering why it is you don't go with me and the boys on our Saturday evening rut. Might be you like the boys a little bit better'n you like the girls. Is that it? Better watch yourself in the shower, boys," he called over his shoulder. "Liable to find this one buggering you next time you bend over for the soap."

"Get off him, Jerry, and let's get going."

Sykes thrashed the air with his arm. Then he looked down at him.

"There's something not right with you, boy." His eyes narrowed. "You're hiding something, or from something. I don't know which, but if I have to beat it out of you... Now get up."

Again he shook his head "I've got no quarrel with you, Jerry."

Sykes went for him then, like a big cat going in for the kill, his powerful hands gripping him by the shirtfront and yanking him to his feet. His eyes were cold. Yet, in spite of the alcohol, they were focused unflinchingly on his eyes. Then, pushing him away to arm's length, Sykes hauled his right fist back and sent it rushing forward. But the fist stopped in mid flight, caught in the maw of another, bigger hand.

"That's enough," a voice said.

He could see the other man now, a huge man shaped like a block of stone. He had black, curly hair and a black beard. Sykes's head did not reach the man's shoulders. This was the new man in camp. The big man did not release Sykes's fist.

"Mind your own business, Somers. This is between him and me."

"I said that's enough, Jerry." The big man spoke with an easy, almost polite, confidence. Then he squeezed on Sykes's fist, but without straining. Sykes's face went rigid and his eyes shot open.

"What say, Jerry? Is it enough?"

When Sykes did not answer, the big man squeezed harder, though still not straining. Sykes finally nodded. "Yes," he said through clenched teeth.

The big man eased but did not let go.

"Good. That's good. Now I think you owe an apology."

Sykes neither spoke nor nodded. He shot a glance at the other men crowded in the corner of the room and then looked back when the big man began to squeeze again.

"All right, Jesus," Sykes said. "I apologize. There. You fucking happy?"

"No-no-no. Do it nice. Apologize nice."

Sykes looked at the big man hatefully.

"Go 'head. You can do it."

But when Sykes did not apologize, the big man squeezed on his fist, this time visibly straining. Sykes, who still had not let go of his shirt, let go then and bent at the knees. Then he nodded his head. The big man eased a little. Sykes looked at him. "Sorry, David," he said, in a pained whisper. "Just a misunderstanding." But his eyes were narrow with hatred.

The big man raised Sykes erect and ushered him toward the other men and let him go. "Get him out of here. And get him sober."

The big man turned away and came back. "I'm Richard Edmund Somers," he said, smiling, extending his hand. "Most folks call me Dick."

He hesitated, looking the big man in the eye a second before regarding the outstretched hand. In the instant their eyes met, though, he saw something—a gentleness—and something more, much the same as he had seen in Carrie's eyes years before. He extended his hand and shook without looking into the big man's eyes.

"You hurt?"

He let go of the hand. "Don't think so."

Then, beyond the big man, he saw the other men slowly

filing out the door, with Sykes among the first to go and yelling that he'd see the yellow faggot Sunday evening when he got back.

When they were gone, the big man said: "If I'm treading where I don't belong, just say so... But were you just going to let that son of a bitch beat you?"

He was silent a moment. Then he shrugged. "I don't know. I guess maybe I thought... I thought, if I let him get in one punch and didn't fight back... Maybe that would be the end of it."

"What? Mean bastard like that. Drunk to boot. He could have killed you with one punch. Don't you realize that?"

He shrugged. "I suppose."

"What the... Whaddayah mean 'I suppose?'"

"I don't know. What difference does it make?"

He saw the big man's right arm move and, instinctively, he lurched backward.

"Easy there, partner. I ain't going to hurt you." Then the big man put his fist under his chin and raised his head. He looked into his eyes a long time. Then he lowered his hand.

"Puh," he said. "I'll bet there's a woman at the bottom of this. Am I right?"

"Could be."

"Well then, I'm sorry for you. But a thing gone bad with a woman just takes time. There ain't no other cure. Not even another woman. But letting another man beat you sure ain't no answer."

He said nothing.

"I mean, the man's a bully. Plain mean-spirited, through and through. You recognize a bully when you see one? Just as soon kill you as spit on you."

"I suppose. Never done too well with bullies, I guess."

"You've run up against this before then?"

He hitched his head to the right. "Well, sort of." He

paused. Then he flicked his hand. "It's a long story."

"I got time. And there ain't no one here except us two."

He crossed his arms over his chest. "Well, my father... I guess you'd say he was a bully... of sorts."

"You mean your father beat you?"

"I don't want to talk about it, really." He'd already said too much, he told himself. He drew a deep breath and exhaled. "Let's just say my father had his ways. It's not important."

"Oka-a-a-a-a-y," the big man replied, obviously unsatisfied. "But what about Sykes?"

"Sykes? A year ago, I would have stood up to him. At least I believe I would. Could have beat him, too, I think. Especially three sheets to the wind like that." He shrugged.

The big man stared at him a moment, clearly evaluating him. "Maybe you could've," he finally said. "You're a pretty fair specimen yourself. Can I ask you something?"

"I don't know." He lowered his eyes, then looked up. "Like what?"

"Like... Just what in hell are you doing here?"

"I don't follow."

"I mean, you ain't like these men. Hell, I've been here just two weeks, and we've never spoken 'til now, and yet it's been plain to me right from the get go that you don't belong here, amongst hard men like these."

"Maybe... maybe not. I don't know where else to go. The woods are what I know. Maybe all I know. It's where I'm comfortable. Now, anyway. And a man's got to make a living. The two just seemed to fit."

"Well, then, if you're determined to stay—and I'm not sure you should—we need to find a way to get some gumption back into you 'cause what I just saw is plain nonsense."

He nodded. "It's complicated."

"Things usually are where there's a woman involved, but

we'll get you back. You have to get back; you know that, right?"

"I know; I know... It's just..." He hesitated. "Let me put it this way. I haven't quit altogether. I know I haven't. I do believe that after one punch I wasn't going to let Sykes get another. So I know I haven't quit outright. But it's going to take me some time to get all the way back. If I can get there at all. And that's the truth."

"I don't doubt it." The big man placed one paw on his shoulder. "From where I stand, friend, looks like the first thing you got to learn is how to care again—'specially about yourself. And trust again, too. You don't trust anyone, do you?"

He shook his head. "Not anymore."

"I suspected as much, soon as I saw the way you flinched there. Well, we've got to change that, too. And we've got to get you out of that rut that you're in. And I'm just the guy," he said with sudden enthusiasm. The big man shook him gently by the shoulder. "You know, when I'm down in the dumps, there's this old adage I like to think about. Never fails to screw my head back on straight. He removed his hand from his shoulder and stepped back. "Care to hear it?"

He could see that the seriousness was gone from the big man's eyes, but replaced by what? "I guess," he said, nodding. "Go ahead and say it."

"Here's how it goes." The big man stood erect, and placed his right hand on his chest, and cleared his throat. Then he looked off at nothing. "Whenever you're feeling lower than a snake's belly in a wagon rut, just remember... The wagon could come back."

He looked at the big man blankly, his lips apart but not agape. Then he shook his head and stood erect. "Adage? You call that a fucking adage? Where in hell did you come up with that?"

"It is a pretty good one though, ain't it? I mean, when you think about it."

"Pah," he said. "It's also pure horse shit." He guffawed and walked to his book and retrieved it from the floor. "You know," he said, chuckling, "it just made me think of something about you—especially after a horse-shit adage like that." Wiping the book's cover with his palm, he felt calm as he looked at the big man. "Given that you call yourself Dick... If you shortened your middle name—just a little—you could have one hell of a nickname. We could all call you Dick Ed." Then he laughed, "ha-ha-ha. Isn't that perfect?"

The other drew back and his eyes widened and the smile vanished from his face. He was silent for what seemed more than a minute. Hurt? Angry? He could see the other looking into his eyes—more than staring. Then he saw him relax. A smile broke on his face, and he laughed, a deep hearty laugh. "Ha-ha-ha. Why you little son of a bitch. You know, I do allow a few people to call me that. And—I—mean—few. Most just call me Dick... or Big Dick. I'm particularly fond of that one, as you might imagine." He laughed again. "You see, though? I actually got you laughing. Did you notice?" Then he grew more serious. "You know, when all is said and done, I got the feeling you just might be one of the ones I allow to call me Dick Ed."

He smiled and wiped the book's cover again with his shirtsleeve. "Well, I'll tell you one thing. I'm not about to call you Big Dick, even if it turns out to be justified."

DAY TWO

4

The first light broke in the southeast, and the day birds roused, squawking and chirping into the cold, windless air.

He looked at his fire through half-opened eyes. Several times in the night he had wakened to feed the fire. It had burned low again, and the smoke, gray like the dawn, rose in a single column. He propped himself on one elbow and churned the embers and then added the last of his kindling. When the kindling was burning, he placed one end of a limb in the flames.

It was a hell of a way to burn wood. Put one end in, let it burn, then move the whole thing up. He hoped this one would burn awhile. He didn't feel like moving right away.

The limb caught flame, and soon afterward, the fire was licking at the fallen tree.

Any other time in winter he would have laid a sleeping fire, like the Indians. A fire long like his body. This puny thing had barely kept him warm. But he could excuse it, he supposed, considering the circumstances and all.

He looked to the southeast where awhile ago a crack of red-orange had opened along the rim of the mountains, and it seemed to him that the sky was a lid being eased back, with light leaking in through the crack. Slowly, the wilderness was materializing out of the darkness, as it seemed he always remembered it, not springing out of the night, but emerging out of it, like the concrete anchor of his old man's rowboat when they drew it up from the depths of the murky lake.

He thought he heard a cardinal sing: "Reet, reet, chew, chew, chew, chew, chew," but the fire was crackling too loudly to pinpoint the source. Afterward, there was only the squawking of the other birds from outside the clearing.

Emma told him that when a cardinal sang it was the soul of someone dear talking to you. That could be his mother. She would return as something beautiful, like a cardinal. It was too bad it would not come closer. It would be nice to have some company. Something bright, with a cheerful song. Not these damn jays and chickadees.

He looked at his damaged leg.

Look at how much he had changed in just one day. 'The first thing I ever told you is that a man's got to be careful of himself. A man's the most dangerous creature in the woods, and you'd be smart to be scared of him.' That's what his old man would say on that subject.

Wasn't that the truth, though?

He looked down the corridor of the valley. With the exception of one outcrop on a mountain to his right, everything was treed. Even if he could not see details in the burgeoning dawn, he knew there were thousands upon thousands of trees, like quills on a porcupine. He was happy about the outcrop, though. It would be a good landmark and, with luck, he'd be able to see it all the way down the mountain.

He reached inside his shirt and ran his hand down the strands of the lanyard. But when he touched the compass, he choked off his breath. He yanked out the compass and looked at it, and his eyes confirmed what his fingers had felt. The back casing was dented, a dent centered and deep, and he knew, without opening the casing, that the compass was broken. That was the reason for the tender spot on his ribs.

He felt his heart start to beat again, and he shut his eyes, but when he opened them, the dent was still there.

He turned the compass over and pushed at the spring catch with his thumb, but when the casing would not open, he drew out his knife and worked the blade below the lid, popping it open. The post supporting the magnetic needle had been driven against the crystal, cracking it. Now the post was wedged. If he broke the glass, the post would fall free.

His old man and grandfather carried this compass for over fifty years and hadn't so much as scratched it. And now look.

He looked at the silversmith's stamp inside the front casing:

1825

MEB

Boston

A hundred and ten years old, and he'd ruined it.

He closed his eyes, and it was like he was looking into himself, and it was all black...

It was a December night as the two of them observed what had come to seem a ritual, ages old, extending beyond them, and perhaps beyond his grandfather, too—their preparation for going into it—the wilderness. And it was in the room where they always completed it, where the mounted heads of bear and deer stared from the walls with the dark eyes that were not so much dead as simply lifeless.

His father took the yellowed and finger-worn equipment list from the drawer of the oak desk where it was always kept and spread it on the wide-planked floor before the stone fireplace that, as a boy, was large enough for him to stand in and where a fire had thundered earlier that night. But the fire was low now, throwing a splash of wavering light onto the floor.

It wasn't that either of them needed the list. By then, even he was schooled enough. And it wasn't because it was December and, therefore, they intended to travel heavy, for they knew how to survive on little and would travel light, as woodsmen travel. It was simply that it was necessary if the preparation were to be completed according to the doctrine that was his father's birthright from his grandfather and, in turn, was now his.

Now he was twelve, old enough to know that whatever his father told him about the woods was truth, and so he did exactly as he had been taught.

They worked on their knees in the orange light from the hearth, the tongued flames settling more and more into a mouthless murmuring.

He watched his father, at times moving almost dreamlike in the flickering firelight, his hands thin, but strong and confident, as they inspected each piece of equipment—the small fire grate, the length of coiled rope, the two woolen blankets for his bedding, and all the rest—and then put each into the pack with the logic that comes with a thousand such preparations.

By then he could do it, too, without watching his father. It was all familiar—the odor of the burning wood, the vacant staring of the mounted heads, and the silence that was always a part of it.

He saw his father place his two, small cooking pots aside. Always his father carried the pots, so it made him stop and wonder just as his father fixed him with his eyes and said: "Pack yours. You carry them this time." His father's eyes were hard and shiny in the firelight, and a look rushed into them—of what, he was not sure—and then it was gone as quickly.

"You not bringing yours?"

"Never you mind, but no. No need for two, and it's time you carried them. You're big enough now."

And so he grouped his pots, once his grandfather's, and placed them in the pack.

The time passed. His father did not speak except to answer a question, and even then only with a gesture or a clipped word or two, until they finished and tied the packs closed, propping them against the fireplace, off the hearth.

The fire was dying, lighting the room as if by candlelight. His father returned the list to the desk drawer, then stood a moment, facing him in the darkness, before he removed something from the desk, concealing it in his hand.

He did not speak, not when he turned, nor when he crossed the room, until it seemed that he had been absolved of flesh and was incapable of making any sound, even his heavy boots falling noiselessly on the plank floor. Then he was standing over him in front of the fire.

"Stand up," his father said.

He did so, looking into his father's eyes as he rose. They were hard looking, like pellets, with the flesh drawn tight around them.

He flinched when his father's hand moved. But he was just extending it, palm up and open, and he could see it—the compass—the silver, inlaid stag's head orange in the firelight and looking nearly molten.

"You seen this plenty of times and know it was your gran'pa's. Now I'm going tell you how he come by it, and how I come by it after him."

His father had pushed the compass almost up to his nose.

"Your gran'pa told me it was eighteen-sixty when this come to him. Traded a new hunting rifle for it. Tried to, anyway. But the trapper that owned this compass wasn't 'bout to give it up to just anyone, 'specially not to no eighteen-year-old greenhorn. Suspected your gran'pa might be one, considering how young he was. So that trapper made your gran'pa spend a month with him. Worked him. Made him prove that he had a right to carry a compass like this. At the end of the month, the trapper took the rifle, no questions asked. That's 'cause there wasn't never no green in your gran'pa.

"He carried this compass close to twenty years. Then it come to me... in just the same manner as it did to him. I had to earn it. I had to prove myself just like that trapper made your gran'pa do. I was eighteen when he give it to me, and I've carried it now more than thirty-five years."

He was still looking at the stag's head catching the fire light when his father's voice stopped off. The stag's head was surrounded by a circle of oak leaves.

"Here," his father said. "You carry it. It's yours now."

He did not move to take it. He could not move, not even his eyes. Then he found his voice.

"No, Pa. I- I can't."

"Take it, I said. Don't make me think I'm making a mistake."

Still he did not move. He looked at his father's face, but his face was the same, expressionless, except for the eyes which, in all the years of his watching, had never lost that tinge of severity.

He tried to speak, but his voice was gone and, in the same instant, he realized that he should not ask his father why. Instead, he extended his hand, trembling, and his father placed the compass in his palm. Its leather lanyard fell like a noose toward the floor.

He held the compass openhanded. He knew even before he touched it how it would feel—not hot like molten metal, but cold, like a disk of ice.

It lasted a moment and was gone, except the question: Why?

And then he felt the words moving upward in his throat again—*No, Pa, I can't*—but it was too late. His father was already moving away. So he stood holding the compass, dreading to look at it even after he watched his father place his hand on the banister and mount the stairs.

Why? he asked himself.

He felt a prickling in his chest. It was the same as when he was five and lost. It was as if the old, dead fear had been hidden all these years in the cold, round object in his hand. And now it had him again.

Then he was upstairs. He could not remember moving. He was simply there, in his own bedroom, with the still unwarmed compass in his open hand.

Carefully, he looped the lanyard over the post at the foot of the bed, and he was aware of his senses once more—the cold run of sweat, the distant galloping in his ears, and his trembling hand.

He undressed and blew out the lantern, watching the light rush out of the room. Then he lay quiet, listening in the darkness, first to his father's movements in the adjacent bedroom, and then to the thumping of his heart until the house was long quiet.

He could not close his eyes for he saw the compass, if anything, more real, and he could hear the quickening of the blood in his ears, too loud because it was night and December and there was no other sound.

Then he saw himself in the woods as a child of five. He believed that his father had taught the fear out of him, and now he knew that was a lie.

He moved to the middle of the wide, too-soft bed and then lay open-eyed, waiting for the night to pass, feeling his dread pound within him.

Then it was before sunrise. The room felt brittle with cold. If he had slept even an hour, his thoughts returned to the compass as if unbroken.

He could hear the kitchen sounds below, muffled through the closed door of the bedroom, the aromas of breakfast already strong in the darkness, and sweet, drifting upward through the heating grate in the floor.

They always seemed to start like that—those days when they were going into it—his hunger pitted against his sleepiness, the bed too warm and comfortable beneath the thick pile of quilts. Always, he'd lie there awhile, listening and smelling. And when he had gathered his resolve, he'd throw off the covers and dress.

But this time only some of it seemed the same—the smells, the sounds of his father below at the stove.

He pushed up the chimney of the lantern and lighted the lantern from the bed. The room was so cold he could see his breath. Then he rose and gathered his clothes from the chair—the blanket-thick wool shirt and trousers, the olive suspenders, and the heavy leather boots. The same clothes that woodsmen wore, he told himself, only he wasn't a woodsman. He was only a boy.

He looked at the compass hanging from the bedpost.

Maybe this morning. Maybe when he went down his father would tell him.

He finished tying his boots and then removed the compass from the bedpost and pressed it hard a moment before he put it into his pocket. Then he blew out the lantern.

Downstairs, breakfast sizzled in cast iron skillets atop the wood-burning stove at the far wall of the framed kitchen. His father was at the stove, but he did not turn or speak, not even after he crossed the kitchen and stood by him at the stove. He only looked up then, an instant. The silence seemed to hang heavy around him, like the steam rising from the skillets and hanging in the still air near the ceiling.

His father handed him a plate, and he watched the spatula move between the skillets and the plate—eggs and potatoes and ham and hot biscuits. The spatula whisking on the skillet bottoms felt like a nail scratching along his nerves.

He took the plate and hesitated, but his father only picked up another plate and began to fill that, too.

He crossed the kitchen and seated himself on the ladder-back chair at the table, and he could feel the compass in his pocket.

Then his father was there. Still his father did not look at him, and there was only the staccato clinks of their forks on the plates to break the silence. And so they ate. Forkful by forkful, the food vanished within him, yet he remained empty feeling inside.

It's just like last night. Why isn't he going to tell me?

Each time he raised his fork, he glanced at his father, but the other only stared into his plate. And then his father said abruptly, without looking at him: "Because it's been five years. Time enough for that compass to pass to you. Does that answer your question?"

He did not speak again, not then, nor as they cleared the table and washed and stacked the dishes, nor even as they loaded the packs into the back of the old truck in the steady, almost-freezing drizzle of dawn.

He took his place on the seat and, after two turns of the crank, the engine grumbled and shattered the silence, and his father climbed in beside him.

The truck lurched forward. Through the rear window, he

watched the white farmhouse as it dissolved into the solemn grayness of December dawn, and then he turned forward, and like his father, sat quietly, staring straight ahead.

The silence lasted. It was there nearly two hours later when his father steered the truck off the main road onto one he had never seen—two parallel ruts of earth running aside a mound of grass, with the trees and brush growing so close along the sides their branches shrieked against the truck as it progressed.

It seemed another hour when the truck plowed into a large, rolling field. The grass was long and yellow and bent with winter, and the field sloped away from them.

He saw it then—the wilderness—a black wall of trees rearing against the gray sky. If the wilderness had a beginning, it looked as if it began there, in the black loom of trees growing larger and larger in front of the advancing truck.

And then it came to him in a rush.

"You're not going, are you?"

"Not this time."

"Please, Pa. You have to. I can't go alone."

"I said no. Now quiet yourself."

"But not by myself. Please don't make me."

"David! You hush, you hear me?"

So he hushed, and there was silence, except for his own quiet sobbing and the sustained noise of the engine.

Through watery eyes, he watched the trees grow larger, until they were no longer a solid wall but single trunks, wet and black in the still-falling drizzle, depthless now and numberless.

Then they could go no farther. His father stopped the truck and got out. But he could not move. His legs and arms were rigid. He could only look at the trees, and though bare, they were like the trees from his nightmares.

He heard the door open and felt the clutch of his father's hand as it pulled him down from the seat. He stumbled off the running board, then found his legs and righted himself so he came up looking into his father's face. There was no expression.

"Don't shame yourself," his father said flatly. Then he took his arm and pulled him to the rear of the truck, where he snatched out the pack and thrust it against his chest. The impact nearly knocked him over.

"Put it on," his father said.

He took the pack and swung it onto his back, almost losing it. His father did not move to help.

He did it again, and this time he caught it and jerked it into position and secured it.

"All right. Now stop your crying and listen up."

His father removed a square of brown paper from his shirt pocket and unfolded it against the rear fender. It was a map, drawn in pencil, with the compass rosette at the bottom right and the hastily sketched landmarks with bearings to each scattered over the remainder. The drizzle made tiny wet marks on the paper.

"This is where we are now," he said, pointing. "This is where I'll expect you to be come afternoon on Friday. I'll be there. Understand? Stop your crying and tell me if you understand."

He swallowed to answer, but he could only nod his head.

"Okay then."

His father folded the map and gave it to him. Then he put his hand on his shoulder.

"You can do it. You don't got to be scared of that."

That was all he said. Without looking at him again, his father walked to the cab.

"But, Pa, what if I can't? What if I get lost?"

"That ain't gonna happen."

"But what if it does?"

His father climbed into the cab. "The answer's in the compass," he said, looking straight ahead. "Now, that's enough." Then he closed the door and, revving the engine, drove away.

He watched the truck, the other pack lying solitary in the back, the very distillation of his father's never-spoken lie. Later he would give him a reason for taking it: "So you wouldn't have to think about it all the way there. You could just do it."

'The answer's in the compass.' A lot of good that did him. The compass was only as good as the one who was using it.

The truck banged and rattled into the field, moving slowly in jumps and lurches, but growing ever smaller until it was just a speck moving soundlessly at the top of the hill and then was not there at all.

For a long time, he watched the spot where the truck disappeared, but he knew it would not be back.

Then he thought about the compass, and he understood. It was not his. It wouldn't be for three more days, or not at all.

He turned and faced the trees and, through his tears, they looked as if they were rearing, becoming darker, colder—bigger even than in his dreams.

He couldn't go in there alone. If he waited a thousand years, he still wouldn't be able.

Then it became too much, and he slumped on his knees and fell into the wet grass and cried.

It was awhile before he got control. Slowly, he got up. He felt heavy.

Good god, how was he going to do it?

He swallowed and shut his eyes.

He *had* to. Father wouldn't be coming back. If he didn't go and *made* Father come back... No, he didn't want to think about that.

Slowly, he removed the compass from his pocket, and after looking at it, not wholly trusting it, popped open the front casing and, checking the map, took a bearing. Then he walked up to the trees and, without touching them, peered in through the trunks. There was nothing moving, and there was no sound. The woods were gray and gloomy in the still-falling drizzle.

Then he entered. He was too scared to cry, and the fear kept his eyes moving and his ears alert. But the woods were quiet. Although he moved as silently as he could, he sensed that every twig that cracked underfoot or branch that scraped his pack alerted some other entity to his presence and that the whole of the wilderness had hushed itself and lay waiting for him to intrude beyond the point of no return.

Still, he pushed further into the desolation of crowded trunks, the compass held open in his palm. He hated the feel of it—its coldness. Could he trust it to point truly, to lead him to the first landmark—a small marsh? And always the tears were just behind his eyes.

He felt that way even when, after trekking miles through trackless woods, he found the marsh. Still it persisted. It was there hours later because the woods were thick, forbidding a true course, and he knew that they could conceal each landmark in a tangle of brush or trees and that he could never be sure until he found them whether he had walked one minute, or ten, too long or too little, or whether they might lie a hundred yards to his left or right. Yet one after another he found them—an outcrop no larger than a one-room cabin and shaped like the profile of a man's head, an open pit of virgin limestone, another marsh with a just-forming skim of ice.

It should have confirmed that his skill, if not his courage, was well fixed. But it did not. Having found one landmark, he was certain he would not find the next and that it was only a matter of time before he became hopelessly lost.

Still, he pushed forward. In the map and compass, he sensed that his father was with him, not comforting—or encouraging, either—but a spur to his fear of failing.

Yet he feared one thing more than his father. And that was the night. He told himself that if he lost his way, he might find it again. But he was powerless to keep the night from coming. He kept remembering the night when he was five.

He tried telling himself that all of that was just memory and imagination. He tried telling himself that there was nothing in the woods that was not more afraid of him and, therefore, nothing that would harm him. But all that day his fear swelled within him as he moved deeper and deeper into the wilderness, and then the day was long past its midpoint and began to wane.

Late that afternoon, in the mist-fine drizzle that had fallen all day, he made camp near a stream and felled some young hemlocks, and he built a fire to dry the ground where he would lay his bed.

Using the trunks of the trees, he arranged his ridge poles for his lodge and shingled them with the boughs as his father told him the Indians had done. As he mimicked their practice, he could not help think of them. Was he even half the woodsman they had been? How could he be? He was just a boy, and a white boy at that.

He finished the lodge and laid hemlock boughs on the dry ground for his bed. Then he settled down, drawing two blankets around himself, and waited for night.

In an hour, the forest began to dissolve into the descending darkness, becoming by degrees the same as the darkness. He kept his fire built up, and it filled his shelter with light and warmth, but the wilderness remained black and empty beyond, and he shook, although he was not cold.

In awhile, he heard the somber hooting of an owl in a tree almost over the shelter. It was answered by another deeper in the forest, a sound like crying, like two women mourning an unbearable loss.

It was watching him. Come to see what kind of coward it was huddled in the blankets by the fire that was too big to be intended only for warmth. It would know that he was a coward and would not stay.

He let the fire burn down. But a quarter-hour or so later, the hooting stopped, and he knew the owl had passed on in the way that it had come, without his even having heard the sound of its wings. There was only the crackling of the fire left and the breathless rush of the stream out in the darkness. The rest of the world was empty and black.

See, he'd known it wouldn't stay. Coward. Well, he would force himself to face it. He wouldn't build the fire up again. He'd keep it just high enough to keep warm. If he could do that, then maybe by morning he wouldn't be afraid any more.

He drew the blankets around him. His eyes felt heavy, but he was afraid to sleep. He stared beyond the fire, and it seemed that he had not stopped staring when the next thing he knew he was waking with a chill, with a sense of amazement that he was alive and unharmed. He built his fire up again but only enough to drive out the chill. Then he settled and slept once more.

Then it was dawn. He felt chilled and unrested and, where the fire had been, there were just smoking ashes. Dawn was spreading, a blush beyond the spidery treetops.

He did not rouse his fire and, for the first time since breakfast the previous morning, he ate a few pieces of dried meat.

He thought it was hunger, that round and hollow feeling in his stomach, but after eating, he knew better. It was the fear, still there.

At least he made it through the first day and night. If he couldn't make the fear go away, maybe he could last long enough to get himself out. But god... He couldn't stand feeling like this for two more days.

He rolled his blankets and broke camp.

For awhile, that day went as the first. If anything, he traveled faster and truer, and the compass felt closer to him. It was still not his. And he still sensed his father in it and, at times, wished he could throw the compass away. But he knew better. He needed the compass, just as he needed all the things his father passed to him over the course of five years. Wouldn't he ever be able to stand on his own? It was like his father was there with him—even his grandfather, the one with whom it had all started. Why did he have to be what they made him?

He looked at the compass. It still felt cold. Then he took his next bearing and moved on.

It was about noon that he realized it. He could not find the next landmark, a small marsh. His father had drawn it on the map and put a circle in its center which he labeled: "Large dead spruce."

What was wrong? This marsh should be easier to find than some of the other landmarks. And he'd held his course.

He turned full circle, probing beyond the trunks with his eyes.

He must have walked beyond it. He'd messed up. Now what? Which way and how far? Think. What would Father do?

He looked at the compass and, when he realized how tightly his fingers were pressing it, he loosened his grip. His mouth was dry, and his legs felt as if they wished to run of their own volition.

He knew what Father would do. He'd walk in a circle to one side of his track. That would bring him across his backtrack. If he didn't find the marsh, he'd walk in a circle to the other side. Was he sure he'd gone by the marsh, though? This was no time for a mistake. And what if he didn't recognize his backtrack?

He swallowed, and he could feel his heart beating.

The answer was in the compass. Fat lot of good the compass did him if he had no idea where the marsh was. He'd be lost. But then, it was already the same thing, wasn't it?

He turned and looked back along his track. The gray sky seemed to lie on the treetops.

He had to try. There wasn't any other way.

He took his bearing and tried to memorize the setting—the gray beeches, the still-leaved oaks, and the rocks—but it was like a thousand other such places. He knew he would not recognize it.

He began a circle to the left. For more than half an hour he moved through the unmarked woods. He held the compass in front of him and took new bearings every few minutes until he had come a full three-hundred-and-sixty degrees. Still, he did not find the marsh and, as he feared, if he had crossed his track, he did not recognize it.

He started another circle, this time to the right. He moved clockwise, as his father taught him. He passed an outcrop with a stand of maples growing from the rock. It was large enough for a landmark, but it was not on the map.

He kept moving. Soon he found a stream, hardly three feet wide—the kind of stream that might flow into, or out of, a marsh, but there was no stream indicated on the map.

What if he followed it? Would it lead him nowhere? He knew the right thing was what he had been taught. If he didn't find the marsh, he would try to find this stream again.

He started once more, but after another half-hour, there was no sign of the marsh, and he wondered whether it existed at all. What was he supposed to do?

He went on, but his pace became slower and slower, and he checked his bearings not just twice, but three times and sometimes four, but no matter what he tried, he could not make the marsh appear and, after a little while, he stopped. He felt the wilderness press in.

He wasn't going to find it, was he?

He was shivering and his heart was raging, and he could not calm either any more than he could make his feet move another step. Only his eyes seemed capable of movement, darting here, then there, desperate to glimpse something familiar—a rock, a tree.

Then he saw it, barely visible to his right beyond the trees. A field of what appeared to be brighter, unbroken light? It could mean an open area.

His heart was racing, and once more there was will in his legs to move. He quickened his stride, though he did not run because he remembered the rule: 'You don't run. Never. Ain't no quicker way to busting a leg than running through woods.' But he never took his eyes from the light, either.

The light got brighter as he approached. Again he resisted the urge to run. And soon it was over. He broke past the trees into tall grass, and there it was almost as he had pictured it in his desperate imaginings—the tall marsh grass, the dark, just-freezing water in a basin smaller than a baseball field and, in the center, a jutting trunk, too old and dead to be sure it was spruce, but definitely coniferous.

He felt a rush of warmth in his blood.

He was found! Good god, he'd done it. By himself!

But his next thought stopped him dead.

The map was wrong.

No, that couldn't be. His father couldn't...

He went over it in his head, once, twice, three times, and he checked his recollections against the map. Ten degrees off, probably more? No, that couldn't be.

He did it again, and again he came to the same answer.

What was he doing wrong? Father didn't make mistakes.

But when did it once more, he was certain. The map was wrong. And with his next thought, he went cold.

What if Father made the map wrong on purpose?

His mind blanked. Then it spat forth the only answer that he could accept, remembering now, both the night of his mother's death and the events surrounding that time when he was five and lost.

He wasn't supposed to come out! He didn't have any idea where on god's earth he was. He only knew what his father showed him—the starting point and where he was supposed to be on Friday. But where was that? He could be in Canada, or New Hampshire, or Vermont. How far was the nearest house, the nearest road, the nearest town? In a day and a half he'd seen no other signs of human life. Good god, good god, good god. He didn't want to believe it. But his father didn't want him to come out—not ever!

He scanned the trees, trying to glimpse whatever it was that was touching him. But there was nothing. And then he thought: What if the rest of the map was wrong?

All the tension seemed to gather into a round hardness in his stomach.

He had at least another full day's walking. And he had to be out by the next afternoon. What if Father wouldn't wait? Or would he be there at all? And if he wasn't, then what? The map didn't take him any farther than the meeting place.

He popped open the compass and took a bearing and moved out hurriedly toward the next landmark—the foundation of an old abandoned inn.

It was more than an hour later when he found it. It was on the bearing his father had written but, somehow, he did not feel any more assured. The sky through the trees was growing darker, and he knew the sun must be low in the sky. He looked at the foundation, crumbling now and overgrown with trees, the remnants of human life long dead and vanished from the land.

If he could just find one more landmark, or two. If he could just know for certain that the rest of the map was right. But it was getting too late.

So he made camp as he had the previous night, and he lighted his fire. He would not let himself build it up. As he sat before the fire, he could not help thinking about the map, and it made him feel hollow and shaky inside.

He took out the compass and looked at it. His father was right about one thing; the answer *was* in the compass, but first it was in himself.

He popped the front casing open and then closed it. There was a back casing, too, but no catch to open it. He put the compass away.

After awhile, he slept but, when he woke, the round hardness was back. It was still there at first light when, after consuming some roots and nuts and the last of his dried meat, he set out. He found the next two landmarks quickly—a decaying log cabin on an abandoned logging road, and another marsh—but the fear remained. And what about his father if he did get out?

The fear lasted all morning even though, one after the other, he found his landmarks. He did not feel the fear leave him until that afternoon. It was as he descended a long, wooded hill, headed for the meeting place. He could see light, bright and unbroken, beyond the trees. And then, like the owl suddenly taking wing, he felt the fear leave him, as if for all those years it was a living creature, wild and misplaced, taken wrongfully from the woods by a child of five. And feeling it go out of him, he knew, without understanding why, that it was gone forever.

He pushed past the last of the trees and entered the field that was the meeting place. At the far end, leaning against the truck in the weak, cold winter sunlight, was his father. He did not wave. He merely stopped leaning and stood straight when he saw him.

Then he felt the round hardness gather again. It was not from the woods now, but from the thought of confronting the dark figure standing in the tall grass.

He stood looking at his father a moment. Then he drew a deep breath and let it out and walked toward the truck. He did not take his eyes off his father.

He'd done one impossible thing, he told himself, and he would face this, too. It all seemed so much like a dream anyway. But he felt the compass in his hand and squeezed it and knew that he was not dreaming. He quickened his stride, still not taking his eyes off his father and, when he reached the truck, he stopped and for a moment the two of them stood looking into each other's eyes. Somehow, his father seemed different. His eyes had not changed.

They were still the same dull, hard gray, and his face was as expressionless as ever, so it was not any of those things.

And then he waited. It would have to be his father who spoke. He would wait and watch.

Finally, his father did speak. He came forward and put his hand on his shoulder and shook him. "You see. I told you you could do it."

"Yeah. You told me," he replied, fixing on his father's eyes. But that was all. His father motioned toward the truck.

He was still thinking about the map, but he did not dare mention it. How could he? But it was over now. Yet one thing was certain: he would never again trust his father.

His father helped him set his pack in the back of the truck, and he noticed that the other pack was not there.

See, he had had no intention of coming after him.

He was still thinking about that as he took his place on the seat. Through the windshield, he watched his father crank the engine. Then he got in beside him. They did not speak, and he sat back against the seat and let himself and his thoughts be carried along by the soft grumbling of the engine as the truck bumped through the field.

He felt so odd. Good, and yet numb. Maybe it was because he could not believe any of it—getting lost and finding himself, ridding himself of his fear, and what his father had tried to do to him. It was too much and he did not want to think about it.

He turned and watched the wall of trees sink into the earth, leaving nothing but the warmth of winter sunshine coming through the side window. There was silence still. He knew now that there would always be silence between them, but he told himself that it did not matter. He was a woodsman. He said it to himself, and he believed it. For the first time in his life, he was something.

He took the compass from his pocket and looked at it, warm in his hand, the stag's head bright in the sunlight.

He could keep it, he told himself. Now he was worthy, too.

He looped the lanyard over the hinge knob of the windshield and let the compass dangle in front of him where he could watch it all the way home...

"Eighteen-twenty-five," he said, as if saying the words would return the compass to its unbroken state.

Over a hundred years and he broke it. Worse. He broke it by breaking the first rule his old man had ever taught him about the woods. He'd been careless. He wasn't worthy to carry it.

Well, he'd get it fixed. No one had to know.

Christ, what was he talking about? Did he actually believe his old man, or even his grandfather, would know he'd broken it?

To hell with them, anyway. If not for them he wouldn't be in this mess. Them and their goddamn thing for the woods. They'd forced this on him. He wasn't like them. He didn't want to be like them, not ever.

He looked at the dented compass.

Still, there wasn't any excuse. He'd shamed himself. If his old man was here, he'd take it away and make sure that he never carried it again. And the sad part was, he couldn't blame him.

He snapped the casing closed and tried to stop thinking about the compass, but he felt empty inside. Then another thought rushed to his head…

How would he find his way out now?

May 1921

The black truck squatted on four flat tires at the edge of the rectangle of rocks and weeds that was Dick's excuse for a front yard. There was not a pane of glass in the truck and, beneath the engine cowling that was crumpled like an accordion, the rusted engine had been pushed into the firewall and was festooned with dangling wires and hoses.

"You've done some dumb things, Dick, but this beats all." Laughing, he backed away from the Model T flatbed truck.

He shook his head and looked at Dick, who towered above him on the porch of the one-story cabin.

Dick's cabin was hardly the model of domesticity. Except for a narrow pathway to the front door, the porch was ankle deep in empty baked bean cans, a prelude to the total anarchy that awaited within.

Dick was rocking on his feet, his hands thrust into the pockets of his overalls. His blue eyes twinkled, and then a smile spread over his face, lifting his mustache and beard around the corners of his mouth. At six-and-a-half feet, Dick was enormous, but he had a happy face, with big eager eyes, and his black hair naturally arranged itself in rag-mop curls. When Dick had mischief in his eyes, as he did now, he looked every inch an overlarge little boy.

"Whatever this truck hit did it in for good. Were you out of your mind or drunk when you bought this?"

"Wasn't neither," Dick said flatly.

"How much did you pay for it then?"

"Didn't pay nothin'."

He waited, but Dick just rocked.

"How'd you get it then?"

"Guess," Dick said.

"I don't wanna guess."

"You wanna find out, don't you?"

"I don't wanna find out that bad. No. You're not going to catch me up in one of your stupid games."

"Ah, come on, Davy."

"Damn it, why can't you just come out and tell me like any other feeble-minded person would?"

"Oh, all right," Dick said disappointedly. Then he smiled. "Belonged to them O'Brien sisters." He removed one hand from his pocket and pointed. "You know the ones I mean. Them two old biddies down the road there."

"No, but I suppose they just gave it to you. Probably wowed them with your wonderful gift for gab."

Dick wrinkled his nose. "Nah, didn't give it to me. Not exactly, anyway."

He waited, tapping a finger on the truck's front fender.

"Why does everything have to be like pulling teeth with you? So... what does 'not exactly' mean?"

"Guess," Dick said.

"No, damn it. I'm not gonna guess because I don't really give a damn where this truck came from."

"You gotta take at least one guess, Davy. That's only fair, ain't it?"

He shook his head.

"Ah, come on. Just one. I promise."

"All right. All right. If it'll make you happy." He leaned over the fender onto the crumpled cowling and looked up at Dick. "The way I figure it is this. You're out one day, hitching your way back from town, when the O'Brien sisters, poor unsuspecting souls that they are, stop to give you a lift. You climb in and you aren't on the road two minutes before you start pestering them with one of your games. They don't want to play. But do you take no for an answer? You just keep after them: guess how many two-cent stamps in a dozen, guess what year the War of 1812 started in...

"Slowly, the truck begins to pick up speed, but you don't notice; you're too wrapped up in your game. Faster the truck goes, and faster. Still, you keep at it, until, desperate, the O'Brien sisters give each other a knowing look. Then, without warning, one rams the gas pedal to the floor and the other grabs the wheel and steers the truck smack into a bridge abutment. Hell, they figure, suicide has got to be better than listening to you. But, alas, a bad turn of luck. The two sisters survive. Unfortunately, so do you. So they offer you the truck, but only in exchange for your solemn oath that you never, ever, speak to them again. And you... You go on your merry way, waiting to inflict yourself on your next hapless victim... That, unfortunately, turns out to be me."

Dick's eyes were really twinkling now. "That was a right good guess," he said, chuckling. "That's not how I got it, though. Wanna guess again?"

"Goddamn it, Dick!"

"All right; all right. So you give up? Go on, say it: I give up. I-I-I-I G-i-i-v-e U-u-p." Dick punctuated each word with the motion of his hand, and he kept repeating them until he acquiesced and said them with him.

"See. That wasn't so hard, was it?"

"So go on and tell me already!"

"There's no need to get impatient. Sure you don't wanna

guess again?"

"Dick!"

"All right, all right." He smiled. "I swapped for it."

"Swapped what! Empty bean cans? They're not worth any more than this truck. In fact, that's where bean cans come from, from trucks like this. Ah, I see it now. You're trying to eliminate the middle man."

Dick looked indignant. "What do you mean bean cans? Why I swapped the most valuable thing in the world. The fruits of my labor."

"And what kind of fruits would those be?"

"Ten hours of cutting and stacking wood."

"Come again?"

"You heard right."

"Oh gawd," he howled.

"Go 'head and laugh, but it was a damn sweet deal. Hell, they even let me borrow their team to drag it up here." He leaned over the rail. "Tell the truth, though, I think one of them horses got itself ruptured coming up the mountainside."

"Probably from laughing," he answered. "God, even a horse can see that dragging is the only way this truck is ever going to move again. Bet the sisters were thrilled having you ruin a horse."

"Hell, they ain't gonna know. You see, the thing about them O'Brien sisters is this. One's near blind and the other's as deaf as a post. So even if the horse bellyached, one couldn't hear it and the other couldn't see what's wrong." Dick guffawed. "Fact is, you could tie them two sisters back to back and still not get a whole working human being."

"Well, if you ask me, you're the one who's not working right. A turnip could see you aren't gonna drive this truck again."

Dick's face fell. "You disappoint me," he said. "Of course I didn't get this truck to drive."

"Course you didn't."

"Absolutely not."

He looked at Dick, then rolled his eyes and let out a deep breath. "All right," he said. "Why?"

Dick leaned over the rail, his hand cupped to his ear. "What's that you said?"

"Why!"

"No need to shout. I ain't deaf." Dick gestured toward the truck. "Didn't you see the mirror?"

He moved back a couple of steps and looked at the small, round mirror outside the driver's door. There was nothing unusual. He looked back at Dick and shrugged.

"You do disappoint me," Dick said, throwing his arms up and charging down the steps. "I thought it ought to be pretty obvious why a man would break his back for ten hours in order to get a truck with a mirror like that."

Dick reached the truck and the two stood face to face.

"Well, maybe it ought to be, but it isn't."

Dick looked at the sky. Then he farted, two loud, short quacks.

"Sounds like the beans are working for you. Or have you taken to smuggling ducks?"

"This is what I get for associating with morons." Dick brought his face up close. "I got it to shave in, of course. Hell, you're looking at what's got to be the finest shaving trucks this side of White River Junction."

For a moment, the two stood, blank-faced, staring into each other's eyes. Then it burst out of him.

"You goddamn fool," he said. "Oh, god, I don't believe it."

Dick pushed him aside. "Just look here," he said. He twisted the mirror outward so he could see himself. "See. A beauty. Not busted. Hardly even scratched. Can't you just see me all lathered up and sitting in this sweet thing, shaving to beat the band?"

"But you've got a beard."

"I'll get rid of it."

Dick turned around, smiling, and rocked on his feet. Their eyes met and he could not hold it in any longer. He erupted in laughter and eased himself onto the running board.

He watched Dick turn blurry through the water in his eyes. "I don't believe you," he said between fits. "Gonna get a bit drafty this winter, shaving bare-ass in a truck that hasn't got any windows. God, you really are a dick head."

"Thought about that," Dick said, laughing. "Figure... Figured I'd have to take it inside."

"But you already got a mirror."

"Not the mirror, you asshole. The whole goddamn truck!" Dick lowered himself onto the running board.

"God, you're even dumber than I gave you credit for."

Still laughing, Dick went back hard against the truck's door, and the next thing, the running board creaked and collapsed with a rush into the dirt, jarring them both. They looked at each other, faces suddenly serious. But then the twinkle returned to Dick's eyes, and an instant later they were both holding themselves with laughter. They clapped each other on the knees until they had laughed themselves out. Then they settled into quiet chuckling.

"All right," he finally said to Dick. "What's the real reason?"

"Hell, I don't know! Why not? Just for a laugh, I guess. I like to laugh."

He smiled. "You're something, you know that?"

"Like to see you laugh, too."

"Yeah, well, you're the only guy I know that'd work ten hours just to laugh ten seconds," he said seriously.

Dick stopped smiling. "And if I didn't," he said, "sometimes I think you wouldn't laugh at all."

He looked Dick hard in the eye. "Don't start on me," he

said. "Why do you always have to start?" Then he stood and walked toward the road.

"Well it's the truth, ain't it?" Dick called.

"Just leave it!" he shouted over his shoulder.

"Have it your way. But runnin' ain't always the answer, you know. You might be able to run from me, but someday you're gonna have to face what's inside you."

He turned and faced Dick from across the yard. Then, resolutely, he retraced his steps until he was looking down at Dick still sitting on the running board.

"Look," he said, bending slightly. "It's not that I won't talk about these things. It's because I can't."

"Whaddayah mean 'can't?'" Dick asked, sounding perturbed.

"I don't even know whether I can explain that." He looked at the ground, then back at Dick. He exhaled. "This is difficult, but sometimes... I feel sometimes that there's another part of me. It's not something I know. I just sense it. It's like I'm only seeing half of me. I don't know what's down there. Honestly. And I don't know how to get at it... You know what I mean?"

Dick touched his knee. "Look, buddy, all I'm offering is to try to help you find a way." He looked into his eyes and held him. "I know this, though. What's down there deep inside you is dark. It ain't the kind of thing you want to find on your own. Alone."

"I know. I just don't know how to take you there. So for now—just leave it. "

5

How would he find his way out now?

The question repeated until it seemed, not his mind asking, but the wilderness itself.

His eyes shot up, glancing at the treetops before his vision rushed through the rest of it—the stark erectness of trees and rocks and mountains. Then his vision met the sun winking above the mountaintops, and that stopped his eyes dead. He looked at the sun as long as he could, then turned his eyes down.

The watch!

He lay flat and pushed his hand into his right trouser pocket. He felt the pocket watch before he pulled it out, and its touch was as he had hoped—smooth metal and glass—but he could not feel it ticking.

When was the last time he'd wound it?

He pulled the watch out.

Seven-fifteen almost exactly. That was right, wasn't it?

He held the watch to his ear, and he could hear the tiny metal heart ticking. He let his breath out, and the tautness in his arms and chest relaxed.

He wound the watch and held it to his ear again and listened to the reassuring click-click-click-click-click.

He had a compass again. At least as long as he had the sun.

He looked at the sky. It was red above the mountaintops, and down the valley to his right there were clouds, but they were scattered, like shredded cotton thrown against the sky. It was still too early to tell whether the sky would stay clear. The only thing he knew for certain was that he did not want clouds—any clouds.

He slid his hand down the lanyard that encircled his neck and pulled the compass toward his face. He unfastened the compass and substituted the watch and put the compass into his right-front trouser pocket. Then he laid back with his arms under his head and looked into the sky. Only the brightest stars were still visible.

He'd scared himself a bit.

He closed his eyes.

When he was a kid... Kid? He wasn't much beyond being a baby. Less than five for certain. His mother had always taken care of his being afraid. It was one of the few things he remembered about her. And having to put up his hand for her to hold when they walked in the dirt road in front of the house. He guessed he remembered that because, after she died, he'd walk like that by himself, with his hand in the air, pretending she was holding it.

He remembered how Tim Merritt bitched about his mother. She ragged him a lot, but mostly she was all right.

He remembered staying overnight. He watched how she put Tim to bed, the way she tucked in the sheets and blankets and then bent and kissed him on the forehead. He'd felt rotten about that when the lights were out because it didn't seem right that Tim had a mother and he didn't. He didn't know how he'd killed his mother, but he had.

He rolled his head and looked at the fire, satisfied that the limb was still burning well.

She died when he was four. Might as well say he never had a mother. All he had was his old man, and what a prize he was.

Most of the time he thought his old man hated him. He couldn't sleep some nights taking that to bed. But when he was older, he thought, no; it was worse than hate. His old man just plain didn't care. The only thing he'd ever cared about, except the woods, had been taken from him.

He must have been twelve when he really started to think about it—that look in his old man's eyes some nights. There was something more than hurt in it. It seemed like he was trying to plumb the depths of his pain. But the pain was too deep, and he never did find its bottom because there was never any hope of finding it.

Her dying was the reason his old man did to him all the things he did. But he survived all that, and the day came that he stopped caring or trying to figure out what his old man felt toward him. It didn't matter. His old man became one more thing to endure.

He slid one arm out from under his head and scratched beneath his beard. Then he smoothed the hairs and repositioned his arm. His mouth was dry, and he touched the split in his lip with his tongue.

But that didn't make up for all the years when what his old man felt did matter, all the nights from as far back as he could remember when he'd have to go upstairs alone and put himself to bed. When he was little, it scared him to go up there in the dark, and especially to walk past their room because some nights he could almost hear her screams coming through the door, and he rushed past into his own room.

He got undressed in the dark because he wasn't allowed to light the lantern. 'You're too small,' his old man told him. 'Don't fool with it, you hear?'

He still remembered the feel of the sheets. So cold. He would climb onto the bed and slip under the sheets and keep his eyes open until the sheets warmed against him, and he'd think about his mother and what he'd done to her. He tried to be quiet about the crying, so his old man wouldn't hear and come up.

While he was lying there, he sometimes thought about her picture on the mantel, and he could see it almost as clear as if he were looking at it. Most nights he could see the stars twinkling out his window. She taught him how to wish on stars, and he wished that he could make that picture come to life. But wishing got you nothing. Wishing was the act of hopeless people.

He propped himself on one elbow and moved the limb so an unburned section was over the fire. Then he stared into the embers.

Funny, the stuff a man dragged around. Most of the time you didn't think it was there. And then it just popped into your head, and you knew it was there all along and working at you.

Wondering about what his mother was like. That was another thing that worked at him. She was pretty. He could tell from the picture, and he could see it in Emma, too. Maybe she wasn't any prettier than Emma, but he supposed everybody liked to think his mother was prettiest. But he figured they were a lot different in other ways. Emma was bossy. He'd always pictured his mother being quieter, gentler. And he liked to think of her as being a happy person. He didn't know why exactly.

Emma was okay for her part. She was the only one who tried to help him deal with his mother's dying. She even did an okay job of being a mother after his old man died. But fifteen was a little late to finally have a mother, and she knew it, too.

Emma had given him that verse. She told him that his mother wanted him to have it, but Emma held off giving it to him until he was old enough to understand it. Of course, Emma wasn't around when his mother died, and he didn't think anyone went into birthing thinking about dying. By the time you realized it, it was too late to do anything besides scream. And he knew you weren't thinking poetry when you were screaming like that.

So it had to be Emma who wrote it down. The paper was all brown and tattered in his wallet, but he didn't need to look at it.

"Far off thou art, but ever nigh.
I have thee still, and I rejoice.
I prosper, circled by thy voice.
I shall not lose thee though I die."

He was quite a bit older when he learned Tennyson wrote that, but he liked thinking his mother felt that way about them.

In all his life, he'd never been able to picture her with his old man, the two of them acting like married people. Even harder was the two of them courting. His old man was working as a carpenter in Bennington then. And there was one thing he couldn't picture at all. But they must have or else he wouldn't be here, and his mother wouldn't be dead. The funny thing was that it was his old man who was the hardest to imagine. Maybe it was because doing that just didn't seem like something his old man would do, or could do for that matter. He wondered if other people could picture their folks doing that.

Emma said that his old man was never the same after his mother died. Maybe she understood the depth of his pain. Maybe she saw that look in his eyes and could tell what he was thinking when he looked at her; like, what right did she have being alive and looking like his Ellie, maybe even sounding like her, and not being her, not being his?

Maybe that was the second most unfair thing life had ever done to his old man.

It bothered him, too, sometimes, to look at Emma. Only he didn't get ornery like his old man. It just made him stop, and then he'd get quiet and try to remember his mother. And then he'd feel rotten because there were hardly any memories—just her dying. That was the thing he remembered clearest and most wanted to forget...

He was in the big room, with the animal heads mounted on the walls to either side of the fireplace. He was on the floor before the fireplace, feeling smaller than the heads. He could feel the heat of the fire on his face and body as he watched the stairs. The room was nearly dark, lit only by the fire and by one lantern, its wick turned low and glowing like a tiny sun in a glass. The lantern was on the table near the stairs.

And he could hear her screaming, and he wanted to go to her and make it stop, but he mustn't go up there. Father said.

He remembered his father coming down, recalling how he turned the wick lower and how the light rushed out of the room and into the glass. And then he left him, taking the whiskey bottle with him, hurrying but not running, walking quickly to the coat tree and putting on his black hat, and then taking a drink from the bottle. He'd never seen his father drink before. He never saw him drink again after that night.

"I'm going for the doctor," he said. "I don't care what you hear, you ain't to go up. You hear? I'll be back."

Then he was gone. He remembered how the night's coldness rushed in through the open door. He was alone then, and the screaming was ringing all around him in the darkness.

He looked at the heads, trying not to hear, trying not to think, looking at the orange pinpoints of light in their eyes—the deer, tawny colored, their antlers casting shadows like tree branches on the wall. And then looking at the bear, the one enormous head to the right of the fireplace, near the foot of the stairs, black, the teeth yellow-brown against its blackness in the weak light, bared in a snarl. So he tried thinking about the bear so he wouldn't have to think about the screaming...

They were looking at the tracks.

"Not a big one," his father told him. "You can tell from the tracks. See, 'bout the same size as my hand. The one at home... its tracks were almost twice as big. This one ain't much bigger than a man. It'll look bigger, though, when it rears."

He felt his father's hand on his back. But he was still looking at the tracks—the big, clawed footprints in the spring mud. He put his hand in one, and it looked like putting a postage stamp in the middle of an envelope.

"So big, Pa. So much bigger than mine."

"Nah. It ain't big, for a bear. Out west, got bears leave tracks bigger than two hands—a grown man's."

He stood and his father placed his hand atop his head.

"Which way's the wind coming from?" he asked.

He waited a moment, then felt the wind in his face. He pointed.

"Right. Which way we gonna go then?"

He pointed in the same direction and looked up at his father.

"Good boy. Remember why?"

"So the bear won't smell us coming."

"Don't forget that. When you're tracking, keep the wind in your face. Animals ain't like men. I seen men couldn't smell bacon if their heads was in the skillet. Animals can smell a man a long ways off."

"Yes, Pa."

He stayed behind, watching how his father moved, the gun pointed at the earth. His father made no sound in the wet leaves. His father could walk without making a sound in dry leaves. He couldn't do it. That was okay, his father told him. Couldn't expect too much from someone who'd only been walking a few years.

They went on through the woods. The trees were still bare, nothing but green and red visible at the branch tips.

Then he saw his father stop. And a moment later he was aware of it, too—the roaring in the distance, coming through the trees.

"Trapped," his father said. "Listen and remember how it sounds."

He listened, and he could feel the blood tingle in his arms. There was something strange in the sound, the roaring too impassioned and furious to be a mere warning or threat—a mindless, consuming rage.

"Damn trappers," his father said, looking in the direction of the roaring. "Cowardly way to kill an animal."

His father went on then, fast, apparently not caring about the noise his feet made.

He was nearly running to keep up. The roaring grew louder.

He saw his father stop, and then he, too, could see the bear about thirty yards beyond his father's motionless form. It was pulling at something with its forepaw—a trap anchored by a chain.

The bear had not noticed them. They were still in the trees, and the bear was roaring at the trap and pulling so hard he half expected its paw to come off. The blood was red against its black fur.

"You stay here," his father said without taking his eyes from the bear.

His father went on, shouting at the bear. The bear turned and, raging, tried to rear on its hind legs, but the chain pulled it down before it attained half its height.

Then he saw the gun leap to his father's shoulder just as the bear was rising again, filling the forest with its frantic roaring in the instant just before the discharge. He saw the bear drop, as if night had balled itself into a black, compact form and fallen from the sky. Then there was silence, so sudden and absolute, it seemed to have leapt from the gun.

He could not take his eyes from the bear. It lay like a burned-over mound of grass just beyond his father's form, with just the flow of red to prove it wasn't grass.

His father was still frozen in the attitude of shooting. Then he lowered the gun and turned.

"It's okay now. Come. You don't need to be afraid." His father extended his hand and he went forward and took it.

Together they approached the bear. He could hear his father's voice above him, barely audible, but loud enough to know he was cursing trappers, saying he wished he could put a trapper in a trap.

They were standing over the bear, and he could smell it—rank, like the smell of a wet dog.

It was so quiet that he could not believe it yet, that this beast, so enormous, so raging with life only a moment ago, now had life no longer. He half expected to see the bear's ribs swell with breath, for the black mound to get to its feet and become a bear again. But after a few minutes, it still had not moved, and he knew it never would.

"Shame," he heard his father say quietly. "Do that to an animal. Nothing we could've done except what we done. I ain't never met a trapper worth dung. When you're older, you ever come across something like this and you got a gun, you do what I done. Ain't right to put an animal through that kind of suffering."

But he was hardly listening to his father. He could not take his eyes off the bear, the huge hill of blackness so still on the ground. Its eyes were closed, and its mouth was closed, too, so he could not see its teeth, and it looked peaceful, as if asleep, although he sensed something different about it. But in his mind, he was remembering the sound it made—the wild, furious roaring just before the gun went off—and then the silence, the deafening silence, the overwhelming silence...

It felt as if the heads were watching him, dusky in the firelight and lantern light, almost melting into the walls except for the glow from their eyes. Never blinking. He wished they would blink, but the staring remained as constant as his mother's screaming. His eyes moved to the bear's, and then he heard the door open.

It was his father coming back, and the doctor, too. The doctor went past him, a black form rushing in the dim light and taking the stairs two at a time, with the screams swelling louder as the door opened and then ebbing when it closed.

His father was stopped by the door, staring straight ahead, but it didn't seem that he was seeing anything. He was just listening, and his eyes closed. In one hand, he held the half-empty whiskey bottle. Then his other hand moved, rising toward his head, but so slowly it seemed it would never actually reach the hat. But finally it pulled the hat from his head. His father stared at it and creased it before he hung it on top of the coat tree by the door.

He came across the room slowly, almost wearily, and stopped right over him and looked at him. Then his father went past him. He watched him climb the stairs, his left hand sliding up the banister, stopping, sliding again. His feet moved heavily on the stairs, making a sound like falling clods of earth. He watched his father disappear a little at a time until he could see only his boots and then nothing.

When the door opened, the screams burst out like lances, and he heard the doctor's voice rising above: "Jacob, get out of here!"

"I'm staying. If she ain't gonna make it, I'm gonna be here."

"Then get rid of that whiskey!"

"No. I can't stand it. I can't take the screaming no other way."

"All right then. But you stay the hell out of my way!"

He looked at the heads again, at the antlers, their shadows flickering on the wall in the firelight, moving like branches in a breeze. But there was nothing in or behind the eyes, and there was nothing in their faces that was like a living creature's. They were not like the bear at all. Its face was frozen in a snarl, and it would be like that forever.

Then the screaming stopped, and the silence imploded.

He waited.

He watched the firelight flicker.

He waited, anticipating that it would start again.

And then he realized he could hear the fire. Its purring seemed to come across a great distance.

He waited, but there was just the sound of the fire.

And then, in awhile, he heard footsteps overhead.

The footsteps came toward the stairs and down the stairs. The doctor was first. They came down slowly, and he looked at his father's eyes in the dim light. His eyes were wet looking.

The doctor's black bag dangled from his fingers, and he had blood on his shirt. "I'm so sorry, Jacob," he said, shaking his head. "She just wasn't made for bearing children. But I told you both. Lucky she managed to carry young David there."

His father did not answer, and the doctor patted him on the shoulder. Then the doctor looked at him by the fire and then back to his father. "Better not let the boy in there. It'll be hard enough on him without that."

The doctor moved toward the door, with his father walking behind. The hinges squealed as the door opened and closed. His father's hand, clutching the whiskey bottle, was the last thing to disappear into the night.

Then nothing—for a long time.

Finally, he heard the carriage pull away, the wheels banging in the rutted earth, hearing it rattle and the wood and leather squeak.

Then nothing again until he heard the sound of glass—the whiskey bottle—shatter somewhere out in the night. A moment later, the doorknob turned.

His father came back in, tottering. He watched him push away the white curtain and look through the window of the door. Then his hand fell away, and he turned and staggered toward him, looming larger in the dim light. His father's eyes seemed to catch all light; they were wet and staring at him as he approached and, as he walked, his father loosened his belt and removed it.

He watched his father until he stood over him, tipsy, reeking of whiskey, the belt beating lightly against his leg. Then his father spoke: "You killed her, you sonovabitch. You and that li'l bastard upstairs."

He watched as his father's hand rose, the belt uncoiling in the air high above him, hanging a moment before it started down.

Then he moved, crawling, trying to get to his feet. He felt the first lash loop around his head and sear into his cheek with an electric crack. He cried out and brought his hands up to cover his face and fell on the floor and rolled.

He heard the belt again, a sound like wind when it moved, and felt it bite into his back. He rolled and rolled, but the whoosh crack, whoosh crack, followed wherever he went.

Finally, he had no strength, no breath. And then he did not feel the belt at all.

Sometime, it was a long time later, he felt the floor come up slowly beneath him and sting against his flesh. And he was able to hear again—first his father's boots clumping on the floor as if a thousand miles away, the floor shaking against his cheek, and then something else. The sound of his father crying, his voice abject with grief, saying her name over and over, "Oh, Ellie, my sweet Ellie. Oh, god, Ellie. Not dead. Please not dead."

Everything was so distant, so muffled, and then the pain oozed into him.

Mama. I want Mama.

He began to cry, crying silently lest his father hear and start it again. He felt a surging cold inside, but outside the pain was hot.

Lying there on the floor, he watched the fire through his tears as it settled by degrees and finally died like the sun at evening, going out slowly, and then just the coals winking in the darkness.

He shivered. The heat on his skin was cooling. His skin was eating coldness and drawing it into him.

A blanket. Wouldn't father bring a blanket?

The fireplace was a black gaping mouth.

He'd bring a blanket, wouldn't he? He'd carry him to bed.

But it did not change.

And then it was past dawn. There was light outside the windows. The room was gray, like the ashes in the fireplace.

He sensed his father in the room, and he gathered in his breath and held it.

Shortly, he heard his father's boots rumbling deep in the floor. They stopped just before his face, dull, and hard, and brown.

The boots moved back and knees came down where the boots had been. He felt something against his cheek—a hand, the skin calloused and scratchy. The hands wrapped around his head, one sliding beneath him, and turned his head upward.

He was looking into his father's face, into the gray, cold eyes. His face was like the deer behind him, nothing behind the eyes.

Then the hands released him. He heard a breathless little roar when they came off his ears.

"David," his father's voice said. "I didn't mean— It was the liquor. Do you hurt?"

What? What was he asking?

There was silence. His throat was empty, but he could feel the pieces start to reassemble.

"Do you hurt?"

What? The voice sounded so far off, speaking in a tone like it was asking the time.

He could feel his throat move up toward his mouth.

"Yes, Pa. It hurts terrible. I—" But he was crying before he could tell his father he was sorry that he killed her.

His father picked him up without gentleness in his hands or arms, holding him like he would an armful of wood.

He tried to speak, but it would not come out.

"Hush," his father said.

He felt himself shaking in his father's arms as they climbed the stairs, and it hurt where his father's flesh pressed against him and, as they approached their bedroom door, he could feel the anguish surge within him. He'd killed her. He didn't know how, but he'd killed her. And then he called out to her, "Mama!" and began to cry. And he kept calling out her name until his father put his hand over his mouth and rushed him into his own bedroom.

His father pulled down the covers and placed him on the bed and removed his shoes. He watched his face through his tears, and it seemed strange to him—dead like the deer.

He felt the shoes slide off and heard them hit the floor. Then the covers came up over him, heavy and cold, aggravating his coldness. His father tucked the quilts beneath the mattress.

"I want you to sleep," his father said. "Stop crying. It's all over. It ain't gonna happen again. You understand?"

He nodded.

"Good. If you hear something later on, you don't make a sound, you hear? Not a sound. You stay right here in your bed. And not a word 'bout last night to anyone. Not ever. I ever find out you told anyone 'bout that, so help yah... You got it?"

He nodded again, his eyes closing halfway, feeling the tears well out and run toward his ears.

"Good boy," his father said. "You sleep now."

Then his father was gone, and there was only the silence left that squatted in every recess of the room and house. He could feel his head rolling, but the rest of him was still, and he could feel the blankets and the pressure of the mattress that made his flesh sting.

It was so cold. Every pore was seeping cold sweat.

In awhile, he heard sounds. Voices in the hallway.

"How's your boy? With all of this, I mean. You know."

"Not so good. Had a rough night. Sleeping now, though. Let's try to keep it quiet if we can."

"Sure thing." A third voice. "This kind of thing's always tough on the little ones. Stays with 'em a long time."

He could hear them in the adjacent bedroom, the movements of men, their voices disembodied and grave. He could picture his father, but not the other two.

He tried to get up. His arms and legs were stiff. He pushed against the quilts, but the quilts did not move, as if they were nailed to the bed.

He heard movement again, stirrings, voices. The sounds moved into the hallway, and then there was the sound of feet on the stairs.

He coiled his strength and pushed the covers off and urged his legs over the side. The floor came up cold against his feet and then dropped out from under him, and he hit the floor hard.

He crawled to the window and, putting his hands on the sill, pulled himself up and put his forearms on the sill to hold himself.

He could see now. His father was holding her blue dress and tiny black shoes, and then the two men emerged from under the porch roof, and he could see his mother carried between them, her nightdress soaked reddish-black and, just before they placed her in the wagon and covered her, he saw her face. It was white, bloodless. And when he saw what he had done, he gagged and, clamping shut his eyes, wrenched his head away—then dropped to the floor and wept into his arms so his father would not hear.

June 1916

Her name was Carolyn Marie Worthy, but the children called her Carrie, and now so did he. They continued to see each other after their encounter by the picket fence. Somehow, without his conscious consent, she had managed to draw him out. He had stood close to her that day and looked into her eyes and heard her speak and had spoken in turn until, without his being aware, nearly an hour had passed. When it was over, he had no desire to withdraw again. That had been replaced by the desire to be near her.

But was it really he who asked: "Could we... Could we talk again?" It was so unlike him. But he took the risk, and how glad he was. "If you wish." she answered, smiling.

She was an elixir. More. She had brought him back from the dead. Yet it confused him, this power she had. What was going on inside? He did not even know where to begin looking for answers. He knew only that some wondrous and heretofore unseen world had opened before him, and he was powerless to pull away.

And yet, strangely, the more he saw of her, the stronger grew his need to return to the woods.

Why? he asked himself. Was it because the woods were

the only place where he had any hope of finding himself, the only place with the familiarity he needed to make sense of what she was doing to him?

And what was she doing?

Nothing really. Talking. Sharing her time and a bit of herself. But was there any real caring there? And if there wasn't, did it matter? Did something exist that transcended the need to have her care back? Good god, what exactly were his feelings for her?

It was all so confusing. She confused him. His father had confused him and confused him still. Everything about life seemed to confuse him. But one thing was certain. He loved to talk with her. She could be so intense at times. And at other times, she seemed even more vulnerable than he. And in spite of his confusion, he was comfortable with her, and there seemed no need to keep bottled up anymore the things that were important to him, that he yearned to talk about—mothers, and siblings, and friends, and life, and books, and art. But only about her art, for it was only because of her that he had any interest in art at all. At last there was someone to talk to, and there seemed no end to the questions he wished to ask, especially about her.

Why had he not seen her until that summer?

Because her father had sent her to a private school in Lenox. Her mother died from pneumonia when she was twelve, and her father, a banker, who was either too busy or simply did not have the patience for parenting, sent her away the following autumn. But she was eighteen now, and in the coming autumn, would enroll at Bennington College.

"Do you remember your mother?" he asked. It was the subject he wished to know about most, not her mother specifically, but mothers in general. Not fathers, though. There was nothing he cared to know about fathers.

"Oh, yes." she answered. "I see her as clearly as I see

you."

"What was she like?"

She looked off at the mountains, as if she needed to reach inside herself to touch the memory of her mother.

"She was wonderful," she said, and he could tell from her voice that the question, the memory, upset her. "So encouraging. She believed in me. And she believed in happiness for her children. What a wonderful thing to believe, don't you think? My happiness would be found in art; she knew that. And she knew how to coax it out of me and help me shape it so that I could believe in it, too. My father doesn't understand that. If it's not utilitarian, it's worthless."

"Who knows what fathers understand! I mean, my father blamed me for my mother's death. I don't want to talk about fathers. Fathers—" But he stopped, uncomfortably conscious of the bitterness in his voice.

"David, do you ever feel about anything so strongly that you know it must be part of your being, your very essence?"

He shrugged and then, because of her fervency, he reflected. But finally he shook his head. "I don't know. Sometimes I feel that way about the woods. And then I think, no, that's just something my father forced on me. He forced me to be part of it, and it to be part of me. Anyway, it's not the same for me as it was for my father. My father and the woods… It's like they were one and the same. I don't know how else to explain it. But it's not that way for me. And you?"

"That's how I feel about my art," she said, "that it's part of my fiber. That I couldn't deny it even if I wanted to. A lot of nonsense my father calls it. He wishes I would give it up and apply myself to learning how to earn a living, in case I don't marry. He's very concerned about that, about my being capable of taking care of myself. Whether I'm happy doesn't matter, just as long as he's assured that I won't be a financial burden on him for the rest of his life. And I'll do it, I suppose.

But I won't give up my art. Not just because I'm so sure it's key to my happiness, but because of my mother. She believed in that part of me, and to deny it would be to deny that part of me that is her. I don't understand how my father can ask that when he knows how important it was to her."

"Let's not talk about fathers."

She looked at him and touched his hand. Her eyes were deep, infinitely deep, and tender. She seemed about to ask him something, and then he could see her cancel the thought with her eyes. Instead she said: "And is there nothing in your life that you feel that strongly about?"

He turned his eyes away and looked into the distance. And then he breathed deeply and let the words out with his breath. "I don't know," he said. "Life has seemed so topsyturvy. I cared about my mother. I still do. I miss her terribly, but at least I know now that I wasn't the cause of her death. That confused me for the longest time. And it hurt. It hurt so bad. And the other things my father did to me... until it got to the point that I wasn't sure what I cared about. My old man told me what I was supposed to care about until I couldn't distinguish what truly mattered to me from what my father said mattered to me. And then he died on me, too, and it was like... like I was free not to care about anything ever again. And for the longest time, I don't think I did care about anything—or anyone for that matter. But it's different now. I realize now that I care about you."

6

He rolled onto his back. With the movement, the aching in his joints and muscles clawed into his consciousness. His limbs, his body, felt heavy, and there was a tender spot on the left of his chest where he had fallen against the compass. All of the smaller pains were surfacing, he told himself: the split in his lip, the burns to his fingers, the other bruises from his fall.

With his tongue, he touched the split in his lip, and he realized it would open as soon as he ate. He could tolerate that pain, he supposed, if it meant getting rid of the one in his stomach.

He flexed his fingers.

They were okay. A little stiff, but they would serve. To think your life could depend on something as piddling as your hands.

He moved closer to the fire. The pain seethed in his leg, but it felt different from the previous day. He felt burning all around the fracture. He sat up and pressed gently on the ridge of bone, and his leg bristled with the touch. He watched his fingers tremble against his trousers. Then he went back on his elbows.

If the gangrene came, it couldn't be for a few days. That was right, wasn't it? It couldn't start this soon.

He eyed the sun pushing to clear the mountains. Then he looked down the valley. The mountains were blue and cold and silent, with the sky red above. He felt a flutter in his chest.

If the leg wasn't getting any blood, maybe it could have started. But what was he to do? He'd just have to push himself. Try to outdistance it. And not lose his head. That was key. Not losing his head. He just had to stick to the true things he'd learned. His luck was in a sour streak, and that was the only way to beat it. By sticking to the true things.

He looked over the treetops in front of him but could not see the valley floor. In awhile, the wind would sweep down the mountains. If it were autumn, the mist would rise out of the valley, milky with sunlight, with the sun a glowing ball behind the mist but seeming to float within it—like some holy spirit.

He looked at the rising sun.

But not today, he told himself. No holy spirit today.

His eyes fell on the crutch lying near the fire.

He supposed he ought to try that.

He grasped the crutch, and it was warm, and he reminded himself to warm it before he set out. The warmth wouldn't last, he knew, but any advantage had to be seized.

Setting the crutch on its end, he pulled himself onto his right leg. The pain clawed in his left shin. He hopped twice to balance himself and leaned on the crutch and waited for the pain to find its nadir. Then he wedged the crutch under his left arm and hopped forward. The tines squeezed his shoulder.

The angle was too severe.

He hopped forward again. It took nearly all his strength to lift his body. Again the tines squeezed his shoulder. He put his right hand between the tines, under his arm. With that, he was able to hobble to the edge of the outcrop without pain.

The slope to the valley was steep and, in places, rocky. He could see over the treetops all the way to the valley floor. Far below, the trees were diminutive, like trees in a child's train set.

Look how far down he'd have to go and at how steep it was. Good God, a slope like that was hard enough on two good legs, but on one, with this miserable excuse for a crutch? He was in for one hell of a day. He looked at the sun, then at the slope again and did not move...

He was maybe fifty steps up the slope, but he turned as soon as his father chuckled. His father had one hand flat against a tree and was bent slightly forward. The laughter came up from under his black hat.

"What, Pa? What is it?"

"Go on, go on," he said, waving him forward with the back of his hand. "I'll follow. But there ain't any animal that'd climb a mountain the way you're setting out to."

He felt his face flush. "Well, how then?" he fumed. "Isn't this shortest?"

His father straightened and rubbed his palm against the two-day stubble on his cheek and eyed him sternly.

"Shortest, maybe. But not easiest. And you watch your tone, you hear?" Then he chuckled and motioned him on. "Go 'head," he said. "I'll humor you. But when we find ourselves a game trail, you'll see how much smarter animals are than people. That is, if we don't die first from the climb." His amusement issued again, part laugh, part cough.

He narrowed his eyes at his father. Then he turned and started up the slope. So what was the right way? How was he supposed to know if no one told him?

He was aware of each step now, that each was wrong. But up he went until he had climbed the better part of a quarter hour and was winded.

"Whatsa matter? You tired?" his father called from behind.

He stiffened, but he did not turn around. He tried to breathe slow and shallow so his father would not detect his shortness of breath. And then he answered in a single breath: "Nope just waiting for you."

He sucked a lungful of air and started up again. He'd die before he stopped.

He had not gone far when his father called out, "David! Hold up! Come back down!" His father was motioning with his hand, but he was looking at the ground.

Now what? he asked himself. But he did as his father wished and went down, grabbing at the tree trunks to brake his descent.

"See that," his father said pointing, not even breathing hard. "That's a game trail. Take a good look."

Running up through the trees was a narrow rut in the dirt, hardly noticeable. It did not run straight up the face of the slope, but traversed it, like the thread of a screw.

"Now try walking that way," his father said, "and see the difference yourself."

He shook his head.

That might have been the first time he realized how much he could learn from the animals, and he'd paid attention ever since.

Maybe he'd be lucky and strike a game trail today. For sure, things would be easier once he got off this slope.

The red sun was above the mountains, radiating long shafts of light that effused the south-facing woods with a red-orange glow. The trees had become trees again—birch and maple and oak, as well as some spruce and pine—mute in the cold stillness of dawn.

"So you've come back," he said, looking at the sun. "Yesterday, I wasn't sure I'd see you again. You've got a lot to make up for. I need more heat from you than I got yesterday. You provide it, and maybe I'll consider us friends again."

If only it was that easy to get what you want. He inhaled and held his breath, then closed his eyes and exhaled through his nose. He kept his eyes closed. He'd save that for last. If it came to that. That would be a pleasant way to go—imagining how it might have been with her. Then he looked at the sun. You could control your imaginings, anyway. And maybe that made imagining better than remembering.

Just outside the clearing, there was a stand of oaks. The trees were still leaved with the brown, leathery leaves of winter, but they were barren of acorns, and he knew the ground beneath would be covered. With his right hand between the tines, he hopped toward the oaks. He stopped to strip a birch of some white, papery bark, which he folded and pushed into his trouser pocket. Under the oaks, the ground was strewn with acorns, and he filled his vest pockets.

Crap food acorns. Too bitter for his taste. But it took time to kill the tannin. The Algonquin would bury them in swamp mud for a year to leach the tannin out. Or they'd grind them and soak them in a stream if they were in a hurry. But the best he could do was roast these and hope to find something better to eat later.

By the time he returned to his fire, his toes and the bottom of his foot were cramped and rigid. He emptied his pockets of acorns, then lowered himself to the ground and eased the cramp out.

The sun was a little higher, the mountains hazy blue beneath.

He moved a big limb into the fire and set to preparing the acorns. Some had retained their caps, and he broke the caps off and placed the nuts in a cluster atop a flat rock. The rock he nudged into the embers with his knife, and soon the acorns were hissing, making the fire sound both airy and liquid.

Satisfied that they were roasting satisfactorily, he pulled himself onto his crutch and hobbled to the trees. Again his foot cramped.

Beneath an old maple, he found another limb suitable for a crutch. As he stripped the limb, he tried to work the cramp from his foot by shifting his weight to his heel. The tightness eased.

With the new limb wedged under his right arm, he returned to his fire. By then, the acorns in the fire had ceased hissing. With his knife, he scraped them from the rock. They lay black and steaming on the leaves as he prepared another batch.

He supposed he ought to eat the buggers hot. Try to keep his body heat up.

He touched one of the acorns.

Too hot yet.

It was only a matter of time before he found walnuts or butternuts, he told himself, or maybe even hickories. You didn't have to roast those, and they all tasted better than acorns.

He shouldn't complain. At least he wouldn't starve. He'd heard about men starving in the woods, in summer. Hell, the woods provided more in summer than his old man's farm produced in two years. In winter it was harder; he'd grant you, but you could still find plenty to eat. Even if you ate the inner bark of a balsam. Not great, but it would do the trick. The Iroquois had a word for it. Atiru-taks, in their language. Adirondacks in the white man's—tree eaters.

Well, he'd adirondack his ass off if it came to that.

Just then the limb shifted over the fire, and he looked up. The sun was starting to climb. There the sky was red but clear. Down the valley, though, the sky was broken by wispy thin clouds, like fine brushed hair.

"Mares tails," he muttered. Although clouds like those at dawn often went away, they could mean a coming storm.

One at a time, while he prepared the second crutch, he ate the acorns. They tasted nutty and burnt, but they were as bitter as he feared. With his mouth so dry, they were difficult to swallow.

He made this crutch slightly shorter than the first because, he reasoned, to traverse a mountainside he would need a shorter crutch for the uphill side of his body.

He was feeling better, almost good, he told himself as he finished the crutch. Here he was, munching away like a contented cow, and he had thought well and clearly about the crutches, and that was good. You could think when you were warm and there was time, even in spite of the pain, and he was pleased because another man might not have thought about shortening the crutch.

He placed the tip of the new crutch over the coals to harden it.

He wished some numbness would come to his leg. Or at least that the pain was not so constant. It was driving him crazy.

He squeezed the bridge of his nose.

Well, there was nothing to do except work in spite of the pain. He had to conjure how to get to Randolph Falls. At the least, he needed to get himself off this slope and onto flatter ground.

He closed his eyes and tried to remember the particulars of all the valleys and mountains between him and Randolph Falls, but it had been too long since he had last visited this part of the Berkshires. And, of course, his map was in his pack atop the outcrop.

Once he reached the valley, he might remember. Or maybe he could piece it together. But holding his headings would be difficult with only the sun. And judging distance... That was another issue. His timing would be off. It might seem he had gone half a mile when he'd gone only a quarter or an eighth—or less. And he didn't have time for mistakes. His leg was telling him that. He'd have to hit Randolph Falls right on the money.

The second batch of acorns had stopped hissing, and he eased the rock from the fire. The acorns perfumed the air like roasted nuts, and he inhaled the aroma as he slipped his hand inside his shirt and drew out the watch and pulled its lanyard over his head. He crawled away from the fire until he was in open sunlight. There he pushed a straight twig into the earth and laid the thick gold watch next to it. He turned the watch until the twig's shadow fell directly over the hour hand through the center of the watch.

It was nearly eight o'clock. South, then, would be at ten o'clock. So southwest would be halfway between eleven and twelve. He thought he was heading roughly southwest when he fell, and the watch verified that the valley was southwest. But a southwesterly course would not take him to Randolph Falls, and he'd have to pursue the least arduous route, and he could not remember exactly where Randolph Falls was. His present condition would not allow a direct route even if he remembered the way; that was for certain.

He sighted southwest and could discern some details on the mountains, including the outcrop he had spotted earlier. He couldn't remember this outcrop from past trips, but it was a good landmark, and he felt pleased as he looked at the watch.

It was good, having the old ways to fall back on. They were true. It galled him, though, that they were his old man's ways, including this trick with the watch...

He was on his knees. His father turned the watch, and now the stick's shadow fell directly over the hour hand.

"That's how you orient," he said. "Listen. The point halfway between the hour hand and twelve—that point is always south. Look."

His father placed the compass near the watch.

"Okay, according to what I just said, where would you make south to be on the watch?"

He looked at the watch. "Well, it's nine o'clock. So south would be— Would be halfway between ten and eleven."

"Let's see," his father said. "Orient the compass."

He did so.

"Okay," he father said, "is south and half way between ten and eleven at the same place on both dials?"

He looked at both, then at his father. "Yeah, they are," he said.

"Then you done it right."

"You mean it works. That's all I have to do?"

"Course it works. But listen up. In the morning, you go the way I just showed you to find the halfway point." He indicated clockwise with his finger. "Afternoons it's just the opposite. That's important. And one more thing. There's just two times a year the sun rises true east and sets true west. If you wanna do this perfect, you'll have to teach yourself to adjust for that. But this is accurate to a few degrees without no adjusting."

His father bent and picked up the compass.

"Think you got it?"

He thought a moment, then nodded.

"Okay. You lead today. We'll pretend like the compass is broke."

All that morning he held a course and found his landmarks. Still, he could not keep from turning every few minutes to look behind. It was not because he wanted or expected his father to tell him whether he was doing it right. During the learning, he knew he could ask for help and his father would teach him. Otherwise, he would just let him go along. No, he looked because he needed to verify that his father was still there. He moved so quietly in the woods, even at a walking pace, that there was seldom a sound to give his presence away.

It was noontime when his father placed a hand on his shoulder.

"Time to eat," he said.

So they stopped in a clearing beside a stream and ate.

His father walked to the stream and drank from cupped hands. When he came back, he brought with him a foot-long stick.

"Before we go on, I'll show you other ways to find direction."

He pushed the stick into the earth. It cast a short shadow, and he scored the earth at the tip of the shadow. Then they sat and continued eating their dried meat and coarse bread and watched the water rushing and roaring over the rocks in the stream. Several times they went to the stream to drink.

When he had finished eating, his father walked directly to the stick and motioned for him to come.

"You see," he said, pointing. "The shadow's moved. Now watch." He marked the tip of the shadow at its new location. Then he drew a straight line from the second mark to the first.

"Around noon, that line, the way I drew it, runs dead west. In the morning, a little south of west. A little north in the afternoon. If you remember that you was eating lunch when I showed you this, you'll remember that noon's the best time for doing it."

He nodded. "Yes, sir."

"All right then. You won't always have the sun, and you'll need other ways to tell direction should you find yourself without a compass. Leave your pack here."

With his father leading, they walked out of the clearing and into the woods. It was at least a quarter of an hour later when they happened on another clearing where there were at least two dozen stumps, the trees no doubt cleared by loggers. With his hand pressed against his back, his father guided him to one of the stumps on the perimeter. They crouched.

"You see the rings and how they're thicker on one side?" his father said, pointing. "That's the side that faces south. That's the direction the light comes from where we live. It might not be true, though, that the rings are always thicker on the south side. You got to use some common sense. In this case it's true because this tree grew out in the open and wasn't shaded by no other trees."

They stood and, with his father putting his hand on his back again, started to walk.

"The tips of some trees point roughly east, where the sun comes up." He stopped. "Like that hemlock over there. Pines will do it, too, and so will tamaracks."

They returned the way they came, and he listened to his father intently, knowing that after the telling, he would be expected to use what he had learned. When that happened, there wouldn't be any tolerance for mistakes.

"Another way to tell direction," his father continued, "is from moss. Normally it grows thickest on the shady side of trunks. The north. I'll show you that, and how to tell moss from things that look like it but ain't. Like lichen.

"Course, none of these ways is dead accurate. But you'll learn to use them good as me. And tonight I'll show you how to use the stars."

That night, before they turned in, his father took him away from the campfire to an open knoll where they could see the stars. His father showed him how to find the North Star, Polaris, first by finding the Big Dipper and then sighting in a straight line from the two outermost stars in its ladle. Those two stars pointed directly at Polaris.

His father showed him how to tell direction from any star just by sighting on it over two stakes and watching the way it moved.

"If it sinks," his father told him, "you're looking west. If you're looking east, it'll rise. If you're looking north or south, it won't do neither. It'll just move flat. To the right of the stakes means south. Left means north.

"The North Star's best 'cause it's always true. But you might not always be able to see it, so it's good to know this other way."

He picked up the watch and held it in his palm.

All the things he'd learned from his old man... If he could shed himself of them, what would be left that was really him? He sometimes wondered if there was anything about himself that he could call his own, or whether he really existed at all. Maybe he was just some mote, some infinitesimal speck, in God's imagination. Maybe we all were. Maybe we were all the spawn of some superior intelligence—all of us acting out our roles as God imagined them. There was a thought! If that were true, then he was powerless to influence how this would end for him. In fact, not even God knew because God hadn't imagined it yet. Maybe God was imagining his life, all of our lives, at this very moment.

Maybe that was better... believing that this was in God's hands. Because if his life hung on the lore and skills his old man taught him, that put his life in the devil's hands. And there was only one way that could end.

August 1919

He was trembling just because she was sitting next to him.

He glanced at her out of the corner of his eye. She had gone quiet and was staring straight ahead. He looked at the children playing at the edge of the park. Was she looking at them, or at nothing? Beyond the children, in the street, a man turned the engine crank of a grocery truck. There was a pop; then smoke plumed from the truck's rear and the engine clattered.

He took a deep breath and released it quietly. It did not quell the trembling.

He was so in love with her. He hadn't wanted to be close to anyone ever again. Not since his mother died. It made him afraid to feel close to anyone. He was glad she wasn't crying now because he came all apart inside when she cried. It made him feel so powerless—just as he had that night with his mother.

He looked at her next to him on the bench. Her hair was pulled back, dropping in a single braid down her back and exposing the breadth of her forehead with its smooth, poreless skin. In the shade, her hair was brown, but earlier, in the sunlight, it had shone with highlights of red. Her nose, profiled against the trees, was straight and delicate, and her lips were thin and as pale as rose petals.

The first time he saw her, he thought her pretty. Not extraordinary. Pretty. Now she seemed so achingly beautiful.

The laughter of the children drifted to them over the grass, and he pushed himself up on the bench. They had been silent a long time, he told himself.

"It's fun to watch them, isn't it?" He motioned with his hand. "Are you watching them," he asked, "or were you off somewhere else? I hate to guess where."

She started. "I'm sorry." She looked at him, then back where she had been looking. "Oh, the children? Yes, I suppose it is."

She turned toward him again, and he looked into her eyes, and she smiled a weak, mirthless smile, and he could see that her eyes were flat and dead looking. Then she looked away. Of course, she was thinking about Wilkey. He wished he could remove all thoughts of him.

Life was ridiculous. She was in love with Wilkey. But Wilkey was gone. In love with another woman—or so he claimed—even if he had gone so far as to ask Carrie to marry him. And then there he was—David Haph—in love with her, only Carrie didn't know he loved her and wouldn't want his love even if she did. But Wilkey? Wilkey puzzled him. How could he not realize what he had had in her?

He looked at her obliquely. Well, if he didn't, David Haph certainly did. What was it that Shakespeare had written? Something about how bitter a thing it was to look into happiness through another man's eyes. How long had he looked into his happiness through Wilkey's eyes? You could almost laugh about it, it was so absurd.

He wished he could tell her how he felt. But telling her wouldn't help anything, or change anything. How sad—all of this love that they had. Love was the simplest thing, the purest thing to feel, he thought—except for maybe hate—but it was the most complicated thing in the world to understand. And impossible to manipulate. And that rendered love capable of making you feel ridiculous and helpless.

Another wave of trembling shook him.

"I'm sorry, Carrie, but could we move to a bench in the sun?" he asked. "I'm chilled. I don't know why. It's not cold, really."

She turned to him and touched his hand, and a shudder ran through him. "Dear David," she said, and he could see that she had sensed his shudder. "Are you all right?"

He nodded.

"I've been neglecting you, haven't I? Yes, we can move."

She rose, or rather, seemed to drift up from the green slats of the bench and then float across the grass. That was how her walk seemed to him, like floating, as if she were more spirit than corporeal being. He walked behind, watching how she moved. She entered the sunlight and then the sunlight seemed to radiate from her and all around her.

"Is this one all right?" she asked, gesturing.

He nodded, and they sat side by side. The sun was strong, but the August air was cool. Around them, in the distance, the green, rounded mountains looked painted against the sky, white clouds piled high and motionless above. There was no sound from the vista, and it gave him the impression of sitting before a mural.

Just then, the children shrieked.

"Aren't they having fun!" he said. He had to think of something to say. He crossed his legs. "You like children, don't you? What am I saying? Of course, you do. Haven't I watched you enough with Nathan and Elizabeth?"

She was still far away. Then she came back.

"I do like them," she said. "Though sometimes I don't know what to say to them. They can be difficult to talk to."

"That's because they have so little to talk about. It's not you."

"I suppose that's true, isn't it?" she said. "I hadn't thought about it."

"I guess I like them well enough, too," he said, "in spite of the talking part." He shrugged. "Anyway, imagine where we'd be if no one liked children."

She looked at her lap, and her bottom lip trembled. "That wouldn't make a bit of difference," she said. "People do the stupidest things—" Her voice cracked.

He sat straighter. What? he asked himself. He kept his eyes straight ahead, and she was quiet, but when he felt her shake against him, he knew she was crying.

He wanted to hold her. If he could just hold her... But what if that was the wrong thing to do? He didn't know what to do. He couldn't stand it when she cried.

He raised his arm, slowly, and slipped it around her and drew her to him. She did not resist. And when she was against him, she turned her face into his shoulder and cried, and he... He felt a great calm swell deep in his core, and then it flooded through his body in an almost-narcotic warmth. He closed his eyes and, for a moment, floated in the peaceful darkness.

"Go ahead," he said. "It'll help if you cry."

"I'm sorry," she said. She sat up and tried to dry her eyes with the backs of her hands. "I didn't intend this."

"It's all right; really." He took one of her hands in his.

"It's just that with Papa dying, and now this. I... I feel so under siege of late. I'm making a fool of myself."

"No you're not. It's better if you let it go."

"I don't understand how he could do this to me. 'You are life to me,.' he told me. Those were his very words. Life! How could he say that?"

"I don't know. Men can be awful liars."

"Don't say that. Please don't. It gives me no hope, and I still hope... I still think that maybe..." He watched as she covered her eyes with her hands.

"I'm sorry. I only meant that... Well... If he isn't a liar, he's got to be a complete fool... I mean, he'd have to be to walk away from someone like you."

She looked at him through wet eyes. "Do you think so?"

"Yes. Really, I do."

"No you don't, but you're sweet to say it." She looked toward the mountains before she turned back to him. "It's not that I really believe that he'll come back," she said. "It's just that I can't accept this. It's too impossible."

"I know," he said, patting her hand. "Give it some time. Hard things take a lot of time, I'm afraid. That's the bad part."

"I'm sorry. I don't know why I put all of this off on you. Dear David. And this is the second time in as many days."

"It's okay. There isn't anything I wouldn't do for you, Carrie." He leaned and tried to look into her eyes.

"I know, and I love you for it. I don't know who else I could turn to. We don't have any secrets, do we—the two of us?"

He felt his face flush. Then he swallowed. It felt like she was looking into his soul. "No, none," he said, not looking at her now. "None that I know of." She made a strange sound, like a stifled gasp, and then she smoothed her dress, as if she needed to do something with her hands.

He shuddered. "I wish there was something I could do for you, Carrie. I hate seeing you like this."

She wiped her eyes with her left hand. "Listening helps. Really it does. Do you think—"

He stopped her with a touch of his hand and, in nearly the same motion, drew his handkerchief from his back pocket and gave it to her. "Shush," he said softly. She flashed a weak smile.

"Let's not talk about it," she said. "I don't want to talk about it ever again."

"It's okay," he said. "Sometimes it helps." He looked deeply into her eyes and, imploring with his, tried to will her close to him again. But she did not acquiesce. She merely patted his hand.

"No. That's enough." She sat straighter and gathered her composure. Then she looked right into his eyes with her blue eyes with the brown flecks. He could see that her eyes were not dead looking now. There was some life there again, some caring, but they also looked weary with pain.

"Are you a liar?" she asked.

What? What was she asking him? He straightened against the bench. His hands suddenly felt cold. He slid them under his legs, against the slats. "Pardon? I'm sorry," he said. "What was that?" He shook his head to indicate that he had not understood, although he had.

"You said that men could be liars. So it made me wonder—do you lie?"

He could see that she was not joking him.

He cleared his throat. "Not to other people," he said. "I never lie to other people." Then he looked away. "I only lie to myself." As soon as he had said it, he had no idea why.

7

He covered the watch with his hands to warm it. Then he slipped its lanyard over his head and dropped the watch inside his shirt. He put the twig into his shirt pocket next to the matches.

Well, he'd wasted enough time thinking, he told himself as he looked at the mountains. Thinking was for people who had time and leisure, and his time was slipping away.

He crawled to his fire and, using one of the crutches, cleared away the leaves from within a few feet. He'd leave the fire burning in case he needed to return to it.

He pulled himself onto his right foot and, balancing himself, positioned both crutches under his left arm. The shorter of the two was of no use on level ground, and that seemed the easiest way to carry it until he was on the slope.

With his right hand under his armpit, he hobbled to the clearing's edge. He paused and fixed on the outcrop down the valley. Then he started down the mountainside.

Once on the slope, he used the short crutch on his right, the uphill side, as he traversed the mountain. Because there were rocks and fallen branches and tree trunks, he had to skirt these obstacles and concentrate on his footing, and his descent was slow, measured in a few inches with each hop. But the land between the trees was devoid of underbrush that would otherwise make his descent nearly impossible. The pain in his leg was hot and steady and holding his leg off the ground only aggravated the pain.

It was almost an hour later that his trail crossed a stream. He turned and looked back along his track and then up toward the mountaintop. He hadn't made much progress. Damn it was slow.

His mouth felt as dry as leather, and the dryness extended far down his throat.

The stream was a few yards wide, but its flow had withdrawn to its center, leaving several feet of rocky bed exposed along either bank. The water was shallow but fast-running, and it gurgled around and over the smooth round stones in the bed.

He moved into the stream, both crutches under his left arm, and was careful to place the supporting crutch squarely between stones before he hopped forward.

In the middle of the stream, there was a flat rock as big as a house door. It rested above the water line. When he reached it, he lowered himself, buttocks first, then turned onto his stomach and crawled to its edge.

He lowered his face to the surging water and sucked it through his teeth. The water felt like liquid ice. When he swallowed, its coldness coursed through him as if mixing with his blood. He felt a stabbing pain at the top of his eyeballs.

It was too cold. It would be worse to get cold on the inside than to touch it and freeze his hands.

He inched back, resting his chin on the edge of the rock. In awhile, he felt the cold in his stomach seep away. He inched forward and sucked another mouthful of water. The coldness made his teeth crack with pain. He let the water warm in his mouth before swallowing, but still, its coldness coursed through him.

Several times more he drank, pausing long between swallows. Still, his thirst remained. The water seemed to soak into his throat as into parched earth, leaving his throat colder but still dry.

He took one more drink, then stopped. It was too risky.

Just as he started to push back, he saw the deer—a pure white doe—and then another doe and two yearling fawns. These others were the same drab brown-gray as the trees and, when they stopped, they became nearly inseparable from their background. But the white doe seemed nearly incandescent against the trees, its skin almost translucent. Its nose was pink, as were its inner ears, but the rest was pure white.

A ghost deer. He had heard stories but he had never seen such a deer. He doubted that they existed. Looking at it now made him shiver. It looked so unnatural, so eerie.

Then, suddenly, the brown doe raised her head, undoubtedly

smelling him just before she saw him. She froze and looked at him through overlarge brown eyes. An instant later, her body contracted before the release that sent her bounding over the hill, with the others following, their white scuts held high as they vanished into the trees.

They were moving out of the high country. He looked at the sky. There wasn't any smell of snow, but he knew their senses were a hundred times keener than his, and it wasn't a good sign. And the ghost deer... That could only be a bad omen.

The sun was bright above the mountains, but it was hazy now, ringed by a corona, and the clouds to the southwest had become thicker.

He turned onto his back and eased himself off the rock. His leg roared. If anything, the burning was worse—so bad, that when he pulled himself upright, he felt dizzy. Just as he lost his balance, he caught himself on his crutches, then stood a moment and waited for the dizziness to leave.

He hobbled across the remainder of the stream, the water rushing clear and swift around his foot. At the far bank, he tried once more to clear the dizziness, but it would not yield completely.

He continued his slow progress down the mountainside, traveling without pause for nearly an hour. By then his hands were raw from the cold and stiffening on the shafts of the crutches. He stopped and flexed his fingers. They weren't bad enough to warrant a fire, he thought. He went on, keeping his pace steady and continuing to fight against the relentless lightheadedness. If he was making any progress, it was almost imperceptible. Each hop covered three, maybe four, inches. The valley floor looked as far away as when he had started, even though the mountaintops across the valley were slightly above him now. But maintaining his balance was requiring more and more of his concentration, and he stopped thinking about his broken leg. And then, with pain snapping in his shin, he felt his left foot catch and refuse to follow. He screamed and tried to regain his balance, hopping on his right foot, but, before he could right himself, he was falling.

He let go of the uphill crutch and grabbed for a sapling as he fell past it. The thin trunk ran through his hand, burning like a rope. Out, out it ran until, at the very end, he caught it.

He worked to get the other crutch under him. The pain in his leg brought him close to vomiting. Sweat beaded on his forehead.

Finally, in short jerks, he got the crutch under him and straightened. The world swooned, and he feared he would fall.

He held fast to the sapling until the pain receded and his head settled into an easy, floating dizziness. He looked at his hand. It was badly scoured. But that seemed nothing compared to his leg. He did not dare move because he feared the pain. A chill shivered deep in his chest and worked its way outward.

Good god, he just wanted the pain to go away. If only for five minutes. As soon as he got off the slope, he'd look at his leg, but for now, please, god, make the pain go away.

He hopped up the slope, propping himself on the long crutch as he retrieved the other. Then he started again toward the valley.

In awhile, he passed through a stand of spruce and then across an expanse of rocky, open ground. Something above him caught his eye.

A hawk. It condensed out of the background of trees across the valley and glided down the face of the mountain. He lost it a moment against the trees, then saw it rising over the valley, its wings beating slowly, without effort. Then it caught an updraft and went up in a gyre without any movement. He could see its wing feathers, like wide fingers at the tips, and the fanned tail.

"Buteo," he called.

The hawk tilted, soaring to the right. Then it circled again, but the wind was carrying it down the valley, and, finally, the trees cut if off from view.

It was a surprise to see a hawk. It should have gone with the others in the big fall migration. He had seen that once, on his last trip to the Berkshires. He watched the hawks soar over Mount Tom. He had never seen anything like that great flight of birds. What was up with this one? He hoped it hadn't gone against its nature. It was beautiful to watch, and he did not want it to die.

He looked at his leg.

He wished he could rid himself of that hunk of meat and soar off with the hawk, like some spirit of the wilderness.

He looked at his leg and the ground that it rested on before raising his eyes again to the sky.

What reason did he have for going on with all of this after his old man died? There was so much that he didn't seem to understand—and he was thirty-five now. Good god.

He searched the sky with his eyes, hoping for one more

glimpse of the hawk, but it was gone—and he knew it was gone for good. There were only the clouds to the southwest now, thin white tendrils beneath bands of thicker, but still wispy, clouds and, above, a sky of white-gray.

There wasn't any secret about the hawk. It was hunting before the storm. How did that rhyme go? 'White mares' tails in a graying sky; before next sun, the snow will fly.' The hawk would hunt. Then, like the deer, it would wait out the storm. That was fine for them. But what was a man to do?

He hobbled forward, resuming his slow pace. He kept his eyes fixed on the ground and concentrated on holding his left leg high. The dizziness circled in his head.

Gradually, the sun became more veiled and the ring that circled it was constricting.

He was certain now that it would storm. Rain would be worse than snow. Rain would soak him and make lighting a fire difficult. But it felt too cold to rain. So maybe that was some good luck. Unless, of course, it snowed too much.

He could not keep from chuckling. It was funny—how the wilderness doled out luck. In dribs and drabs. Sometimes good. Then bad. Then maybe all good for a long time or all bad—like the card games in Winslow's back room. He'd never tempted luck, except one time maybe. That time he'd gone into the woods without anything, not even the compass. The wilderness wasn't like an animal or man, though. You couldn't bait it. To this day he wasn't sure what he had been trying to prove. That he was better than the wilderness? Or maybe it was just the nagging. After all those years, the nagging memory of that night in the woods and the fear that he had carried afterward was still working at him. And when he dreamed about it... Maybe that was it. Maybe he was trying to rid himself of the dream.

But what was he going to do now? He couldn't toss in his cards and quit. And he couldn't raise the stakes. This was it. The last hand... and what had he proved or learned about himself? He had waited thirty years, and for this? The only thing he'd proved was that the wilderness could out-wait him. And why not? It had all the time in the world for him to make a mistake.

He stood and took his weight off the crutches and rubbed his armpits. The rubbing eased the stiffness in his fingers, but several times he wavered left, then right.

Damn his head.

He looked at the outcrop. It was slightly above him. He checked his watch.

Maybe a quarter of a mile in a bit more than three hours. By his judgment, there was still at least three or more hours before he was off the slope. He wasn't going to make much distance. Why couldn't he have broken an arm, or a rib? If it rained or snowed heavily, that was it.

Gradually, over the next several hours, the slope eased and using the crutches became easier. But then the ground leveled and the going became difficult because the right crutch was too short.

He entered an open area and pushed into it. Here the valley floor was a sheet of gray granite. There were a few barren trees here and there. Beyond them, on his right, three tree-covered knolls bulged.

He hopped to the first mound and, there, rested on a fallen tree near a jagged protrusion of granite. At the top of the mound, a stand of pines rose green, almost black, against the gray sky.

When he was well rested, he gathered firewood from around the knoll, hobbling on only the longer of the crutches. He piled the wood higher than his knees. Then, with his back against the granite rock, he made a tepee from some twigs and some birch bark from his pocket. He started his fire with one match.

He thought about eating some more of the acorns, but his throat was so dry he knew he could not swallow them.

He had neglected to look for food. How could he have forgotten that? It was his head. He could still think, but he had concentrated so hard on not falling that he had forgotten everything else. Maybe if he rested awhile the dizziness would go.

He eased back against the granite, trying to relax and warm himself. Soon the fire was burning well and penetrating the cold of his hands and body. The sky was solid gray, not a dark, foreboding gray, but brooding lower and lower and making the mountaintops ghostly through its scud.

The burning in his leg was incessant. He repositioned the leg, feeling the muscles bunch in his thigh as he raised the leg off the ground. It did not help the burning.

Hadn't he told himself he was supposed to check his leg?

He slipped one finger under the laces of the splint. The pain leapt. The splint had not moved, and he was sure that he had not tied it so tight that it would cut off the circulation.

He leaned back and drew a deep breath. When he exhaled, it came out of him shaking.

He supposed he ought to take the splint off and look.

He felt a run of saliva in his mouth, sharp and brassy. His fingers trembled at the knots, and the pressure of leaning forward made the pain almost unbearable.

The first knot came free, and then the second.

He took the splint away cautiously and placed it beside him and wiped away the sweat from his forehead. His trouser legs were loose fitting normally, but he could see a difference. The fabric against his left shin and calf was almost tight. He turned his head away and slowly inched the trouser leg up. When he looked back, his stomach tumbled. The entire lower leg was black and incredibly swollen. There was the protruding ridge of bone, and the green-black oblong that surrounded it and the purplish red beyond. And there was something that he had not expected. Was his leg blistering?

There was no smell, but he knew well enough.

He covered his mouth with his hand and turned his head away. His stomach convulsed. He folded his arms and pressed hard against his chest. Then he tipped himself onto his right side and his stomach constricted.

The fire was hardly burning when he finally felt the constrictions ease, but the push, push, pushing had thrust nothing out of his mouth except remnants of acorns and its own agonized convulsions.

Now he felt spent. He wiped the water from his eyes.

It was so big. How was it possible to swell to a size like that? My god, what had he done to himself?

He rolled onto his back. His head felt both leaden and dizzy as it followed his body. There was a hollowness inside him, and he was shivering. The shivering started at the center of the hollowness and shook its way out.

He rolled onto his stomach, looking for the fire. His body felt far away and dreamlike as he moved until his forehead smacked against the ground. Then his eyes shot open, and he could see that he was already next to the fire.

He reached out, dribbling his hand to the woodpile, and tugged out a stick and churned the embers. Then he pulled out several pieces of wood and let them topple into the fire. When he stopped moving, the cold clutched him and shook him, and the back of his neck bristled. And then he felt what he had the previous day. That something was watching him.

He pushed himself onto one elbow and searched with his eyes, starting from where he had emerged from the mountainside and turning his head until he was looking past the knolls, down the barrel of the valley. In the distance, the trees rose again, a dark wall beneath the gray clouds. He saw nothing, but he could feel his blood quicken, and he could feel the silence yawning up the valley and pushing into him. What was he sensing? Whatever it was, it was touching him now, with cold probing fingers. Was it death? Was this how it would be, with death stealing his soul away in little snatches?

Suddenly, he felt a white heat at his core. It surged to his face and head.

Why wasn't there anything for this? he asked himself irately. He felt the heat still rising within him. Out of all the things his fucking old man had taught him, why wasn't there anything for this? And why did it always come back to him? Goddamn it! Enough! It was enough! He was through with him! Through! "Oh, you son of a bitch," he shouted.

He thrust his hand into his pocket and yanked the compass out and looked at it, feeling hot strands tighten in his chest. And when he could not keep it contained any longer, he shouted at the sky: "Fuck you! Burn in hell! I'm through with you! Through!" And then, openhanded, he smashed the compass against the rock. He smashed it and smashed it and smashed it, all the time repeating: "Through! Through! Through!"

With each blow, he felt the anger flow out of him, out through the flesh and bone of his driving hand and into the small, compact object that it labored to destroy without any hope of destroying it absolutely. On he went until the casing broke apart against his hand. Then, abruptly, he stopped. He left the compass on the rock without looking at it. Then he wept quietly, all the time repeating, "through," until his voice, of its own hopelessness, dwindled into silence.

After awhile, he looked up. The sky was blurry. He looked at the compass lying smashed on the rock, and he saw something. A speck of yellow-brown. He wiped his eyes. There it was, just visible inside the sprung back casing.

He picked up the compass and pulled back the casing, and then he saw that there was a false casing beneath that, sprung too by the pummeling. But what was it? He pulled back the second casing. It was a folded piece of paper.

He licked his dry lips and stared at the paper. Once more he dried his eyes. He removed the paper carefully. The blood pounded at his temples.

Who put it there—his grandfather? The old trapper? Maybe it was the original receipt.

He held the paper in his open palm and then, swallowing, he wiped his eyes again and carefully began to open the paper. It was so brittle that it split along one crease. He opened the next fold, and then the next. There was only one more fold.

He stopped. His heart was driving like an engine. He closed his eyes as he opened the last fold. When he looked, there it was—the last thing he wanted, or expected, to see: a block of writing in the squat, bold letters of his father's hand.

He read the first sentence and stopped. He felt his heart leap and surge into a more rapid beating. His hand, fell like dead weight into his lap. "No," he said. "No-no-no-no-no." And then at nothing: "No!"

August 1905

He was in the dirt road in front of the house, and he was pulling crabapples from the one tree that grew beside the road. He had to climb the fence rails to reach the apples and then climb down again to throw them at the posts.

Around him, the land was still, the air thick with heat, almost viscous, with one lonely elm in the adjacent pasture pasted, drooping, against the milky sky. The sun burned through the haze and was hot on his bare arms.

He had just climbed down when he heard the engine clattering out of the hot, shimmering distance. He heard it long before he could see the black automobile's compact form, seemingly wheelless, bouncing above the long grass of the pasture.

Then it was close enough for him to see, and, when he saw her, the apples dropped from his hands.

Mama! Was it Mama?

The driver squeezed the bulb horn twice as the automobile rattled past, a storm of shivering black steel and billowing dust. It negotiated the last ruts in front of the white house and stopped, then rolled back, backfiring as the engine shuddered silent. The dust thinned slowly and finally settled.

He could feel the frantic leaping against his ribs as the woman on the passenger's side turned and waved to him.

Mother! he exclaimed to himself, and then he was running, trying to scramble onto the running board that was too high, but when the door opened, he backed off and looked up as the woman stepped down. His eyes, wide and eager now, devoured her, her brown hair drawn in a neat bun to the back of her head, the pretty, young face, oval and sharp at the chin, and her eyes clear blue but warm-looking in the sunlight. It was; it was Mother, just as he remembered her.

"Mama!" he yelled, running into her arms. "You're back! You're back!"

Her arms came around him, and one of her hands pressed against the back of his head and drew him to her cheek. "Oh, Sweetheart," she said. "No. No. It's not your mum, dear. It's Aunt Emma."

He pushed away from her, feeling the elation sink within him. He studied her face.

"I know you don't remember," she said. "You were just a baby last time I saw you."

The leaping in his chest became leaden. "Not Mama?"

"No, Sweetheart, no. Not your Mama."

He looked at her and bit hard on his lip. She looked like her. Pretty like her. He started to cry.

She reached to him then and tried to cradle him in her arms, but he pushed away. "No!" he said. "Go away! I don't want it to be you!"

She tightened her hold against his struggling. "I know, I know," she said. "Easy child. Easy."

"No! Let go! You're not my mother!"

She let go, and he backed off.

"I don't want it to be you," he said. His eyes were hot with tears.

Then her eyes became glassy, and he saw tears at the corners. He heard a door close and saw the driver, a tall man wearing goggles and a flat hat with a small visor and a long canvas duster, walking around the front of the automobile. He stopped behind the woman.

"Sweetheart, come here," the woman said softly. "Aunt Emma wants to talk to you."

But he did not move. He was still looking, feeling his heart clamoring against the impossible lie he beheld with his eyes. Then he looked at the man whose goggles made his face look like the frogs' in the pond near the farm.

And then she said it more firmly: "David, come here I said. Please."

He hesitated, but then went to her, scuffing his shoes in the dirt and not looking at her. She lifted his chin with her fingertips and dabbed at his eyes with a handkerchief.

"Look at me, Sweetheart."

He did. Her eyes were still wet looking.

"Sweetheart, if I could make it be your mother, don't you know I would? Aunt Emma would give anything to be able to do that for you. But I can't, and there isn't anything I can do to make her come back. Nothing anybody can do."

"But why? Why can't she come back?" His bottom lip was trembling, and he could feel tears starting in his eyes again.

"Oh, darling, how can I make you understand that?"

"I did it. I made her go away."

"Oh, lord, child. Of course you didn't." She drew him to her. "Where did you ever get that idea?"

"I don't want her to be gone, Aunt Emma! I don't!"

"I know, child. I know. I don't either," she said. with her voice breaking. "But she's not really gone, you know."

"She is, too," he said hopelessly.

"No-no, she's not."

"Where is she then?" he demanded.

"Well, you and I can't see her, but she's here, watching you. Believe me. And you know what? It makes her sad to see you so unhappy."

"How come? If she's here, how come I can't see her?" He pushed away and looked at her.

She turned her eyes up and tried to blow a lock from her forehead. Then she looked at him again.

"Stop your crying and Aunt Emma will see whether she can make you understand. Can you do that?"

He nodded and smeared his eyes with the backs of his hands.

"Good boy. Now you just do what I tell you, okay?"

He nodded.

"Good. Now, the first thing I want you to do is put your hands over your eyes so you can't see me."

"Like in hide'n'seek?"

"That's right. Just like in hide and seek."

He covered his eyes with his hands.

"Can you see me now?" she asked.

"Unh-unh."

"You can't see me, but I'm still here, aren't I? You know because you can hear me. Right?"

He nodded.

"Okay. Listen close now. I want you to shut your eyes real tight." She paused. "Are they shut tight?"

"Yes."

"All right. Aunt Emma is going to move your hands. I'm just going to put them over your ears. After I do, I want you to listen extra careful because I'm going to say something to you. I want you to tell me what I say. No cheating, though. Keep your ears covered real tight until I tell you. Okay?"

"Okay, I guess."

When she moved his hands, the black behind his eyelids

became bright. She guided his hands to his ears, and then he pressed his hands hard. There was a low roaring and rumbling inside his head. He stood like that until, a few moments later, he felt her hands on his wrists.

"Okay," she said. "Did you hear what I said to you?"

He shook his head. "No. I didn't hear anything."

"But you knew that all the time Aunt Emma was right here next to you, didn't you?"

He nodded. "Yes."

She crouched and put her arms around him and his chin rested on her shoulder. He liked the way she smelled, like flowers.

"That's kind of the way it is between you and your mum now. Dying is something like that. Like someone has put something over your eyes and ears that keeps you from seeing or hearing the other person. Just like you couldn't see or hear me. But you know, all the time that you couldn't see or hear me, I could still see and hear you. And that's the way it is for your mum. She can still see you. And hear you. And she loves you so very much."

He pulled back and looked her in the eye.

"Really?" he said. "It's not a lie?"

"Nope. Honest injun. That's why you mustn't be so sad. Just remember that your mum is always with you even though you can't see her. And any time you want to talk to her, she'll hear you."

"Even now?" he said, the tears starting in his eyes again. She didn't look like she was lying.

"Yes, even right now."

"Oh, Mama," he cried, "I'm sorry I made you go away."

8

All he could see were those frightened eyes looking up at him. But it was too late. His foot had already started forward. It hit the ground in an explosion of dirt before his boot smashed into his father's face.

After that, there wasn't anything. His father's head, shaking, slowly pulled out of the dust and turned upward. And then there was just the two of them looking at each other, looking and looking in the awful silence, his father struggling to keep his head up. He remembered how those eyes filled then, with a look so anguished it made him regret the act immediately. But too late. At the very instant of his regretting, the life died in his father's eyes and his head dropped into the dirt.

He stood a moment, anchored yet adrift in the unbearable silence, and it seemed that the world and everything in it had been kicked into dumbness, while the regret surged and transformed within him—bubbling, erupting, first into remorse, then finally into grieving.

"Oh god, Pa." he cried. He bent and clawed at the body, trying to turn it over. Finally, by clutching one of the gaunt shoulders and pulling, over the body came, the face all covered with dust, the gray eyes still open but showing nothing of surprise or anguish now. They were empty, unseeing, different from the eyes of the trophies on the walls because these were the windows into the life just departed.

"Oh god, Pa, I'm sorry." he cried. He grabbed the straps of the blue overalls and pulled his father's body up and shook it. "Please don't be gone. Please. Not you, too." Oh, god, what had he done?

"Pa.

"Pa!

"Pa!"

And then, abruptly, he stopped. He looked a moment into the dead eyes, and it startled him at the difference now that there was no life. He lost his grasp and his father's body dropped into the dirt. He rose and looked down at it, his chest tightening, the emotion surging to his throat.

"No! No!" he bellowed at the sky. Tears filled his eyes. And then he turned to his father: "Damn you! I'll hate you forever. So help me god, I swear I will."

And then he had to run. The impulse pushed into his legs. He charged across the yard and took the steps in one leap, crashing into the back door of the house and sending it slamming into the wall. Its one large pane of glass shattered and crashed to the floor.

He rushed into the kitchen. There he was riveted at the center of the floor as he pivoted full circle on one foot. "Damn you!" he screamed. "Both of you! I don't need you. I don't need either of you!"

The urge that had moved into his legs was coursing into his arms now, his hands. He hunted the kitchen, and then he saw them—the blue and white checked curtains above the pump at the sink, and in an instant he was on them, twisting his hands into the fabric and wrenching the curtains from the window. He twisted and bent the rod and then crumpled the curtains into a ball and, bellowing, hurled them against the wall.

Again he hunted with his eyes. Through the doorway to the big room he rushed. He saw the white curtains in the double windows along the wall. He sprang and sank his fingers into the first pair, wrapping his hands in them and tearing them from the window. But when they were down, the view from the window was unobstructed, and he looked out and saw his father's body lying in the yard, the head turned toward the house, the eyes fixed, as if staring in horror at the violation occurring inside.

He cried out and tried to free his hands, but they were well tangled, and in his frenzy, his fist suddenly flew free, smashing the window.

He ran again, leaving the curtain still hanging in the other window, desperate to get away from the vision in the yard.

He ran the length of the living room, past the mounted heads, oblivious to their stares.

At the white, transparent curtain of the front door, he stopped. Again he felt the urgency thrusting into his arms. The curtain, fastened by rods at the top and bottom, shredded under his clawing, and when he could get his fingers through the fabric, he tore the curtain away, not even hesitating before he rushed to the curtain in the adjoining window, tearing it down, too, and then the curtain in the window next to that, the last. He wound his hands in the fabric and wrenched it free. It flew from the wall, and the rod struck him on the forehead. The blow stopped him short.

He stood before the window, staring out through his tears. Just beyond the roof of the porch, he could see the sky, hazy and white with heat.

Oh god, how could he have? And now he could never take it back. Oh god, help him.

He turned away from the window and pressed himself into the corner and, when he felt the abutting walls against his back, he let his feet go out from under him, and his back slid down the walls.

He wanted to die. Please, god, just let him die, too.

He closed his eyes.

What in god's name was he going to do now? he asked himself, and then he buried his face in the curtain.

He was still there that evening when Vern DeNault, a neighbor, stopped to return a harness.

He stared at the note, not reading it. The words were a blur, but the images from the day of his father's death, so long repressed, repeated in his mind, horrible in their clarity, as if being played out for the first time on the yellow sheet in his hand.

He roused himself and wiped his eyes and read the note again:
    "David

        Didn't do this out of no meanness. If you be reeding this, I'm disappointed. It means you didn't believe none in yourself cause I know I showed you good enough how to get out from being lost. Did this cause there's only one way I know to get rid of being scared, and that's to face up to what scares you. Had to make you do that so you could have a clear shot at becoming a man. So you could live with yourself without no taint. That's all I'm going to say on it. To get yourself out, head due west to you come to route 7. Runs the length of the state, so you can't help run into it. Be about a days walk. Get yourself to Brandon. If you don't come out where you was supposed to, I'll get you in Brandon next day or the day after. Go to Clinton's General Store. You tell Luke Clinton your my son. He'll tend to you."

He read the note again, unable to keep from rereading the impossible words: 'Didn't do this out of no meanness.'

No! he insisted to himself. It was a lie. He'd done it to cover himself; that was all. When the searchers found his body, his old man could just point to the note, "Read it. Just read the note. It proves I wasn't trying to kill him." It couldn't be the truth. It just couldn't.

He looked up from the yellow sheet, and his eyes fixed on the compass lying smashed on the rock, and he remembered his father's words from so long ago: "The answer's in the compass."

Good god. In all his wildest imaginings, it never occurred to him that this was what he meant. Son of a bitch. Why couldn't he just talk to him like a normal person? No, don't say any more than you have to. Don't even say enough so that a body could understand what was true. "The answer's in the compass." Then just get in the fucking truck and drive away. He'd thought he was telling him he'd have to rely on himself, on his own abilities using the compass. How the hell was he supposed to think otherwise?

Damn him! He had him again. He'd no sooner broken with the son of a bitch when he had him again. Why wouldn't he just let go?

He looked at the compass, and then at the note, and then at the compass. It felt like something had exploded inside of him and that there was nothing left in there now, all of it wasted and empty.

Good god, what was the truth? Had his whole life been a lie?

No. No. That wasn't right, either. His old man was a son of a bitch. Time after time. Hadn't he blamed him for his mother's death? Hadn't he beaten him to a pulp? Hadn't he left him in the woods when he was five? Oh, god, he didn't know. Maybe he had deluded himself, convinced himself that there couldn't possibly be anything good about his old man. Was it all a lie?

He shook his head hard, trying to rid himself of thought, but images pushed upward, seeping out of the darkness…

Shaking, he looked over the flames, past his father, but there was nothing but darkness. Even the trees were invisible, as if the fire had shrunk the world to a tiny circle, beyond which nothing existed, not the world, nor the wilderness, nor the farm, but only the night. His father seemed not to be completely there, either, just his face, pasted bright like a moon against all the blackness.

Then his father turned and set his hat beside him on a log, and with the movement he became whole again.

The wind moaned low somewhere far out in the darkness, barely audible above the sound of the fire.

"Your gran' pa. Brung me here my first time, too," his father said. "He sat here, where I'm sitting now, on this rock, and I sat where you are."

His father looked past him or, for a moment, was not looking at anything. There was an odd look in his eyes, like sadness, but it might have been just the fire doing it.

"Why here, Pa?"

His father's eyes came back. "Don't know. Good a place as any, I guess. Long as it was in the woods. Probably no more than that. Know why he brung me, though. Same reason I brung you."

His father sat up straight and patted both coat pockets with his hands. Then he reached into the right pocket and took out his tobacco pouch and corncob pipe.

"Why, Pa?"

"I'm coming to it, I'm coming." He ran his little finger around the inside of the bowl, then tilted the pipe toward the fire. In the firelight, his face looked gaunt, all shadow and light and angles. The stubble that always seemed to be there, even after he just shaved, caught the light in flecks along his chin.

Finally, he sat back and loaded the pipe and lit it with a stick from the fire. Then, puffing, he looked at him over the flames, an easy, unhurried look, and blew out the flaming stick.

"You don't recollect nothing of your gran' pa," he said. "You was just a snip when he died. Too bad. You see, your gran' pa started something here with me forty years ago. And, well, if he was still alive, he'd be telling you the same things he tole me."

He drew several times on his pipe, his lips popping softly.

"What did he say, Pa?"

His father put up his hand, which meant for him to hush.

"Tole me he brought me here to start me on learning two

things. Said they was the only two things worth knowing in this life. I was about eight then, I guess. "Bout the same age as you. But he thought that that was old enough. You know what those two things are?"

He shook his head.

"Well, maybe some day you'll bring your boy here, too," his father said. "'Cause this spot is part of it. Your heritage. That's what your gran' pa called it. It was his word. And that's one of the things he told me about. Heritage. Knowing where it is you come from, that you weren't just born with nothing behind you." His father motioned with his pipe. "How 'bout throwing a couple of them pieces on."

He stood and pulled two pieces of wood from the pile he had laid and placed them on the fire. He sat again.

"It's a good sounding word, ain't it, that word heritage? This spot... fact, these woods; they're part of yours. Mine and your gran' pa's, too. Ain't none of us knows just where we're heading in this life. That's what he tole me. But knowing where it is you come from... That can make it a whole lot easier on the road to wherever it is you gonna end up."

His father chuckled and shook his head, and then his eyes were far away again, looking at nothing.

"Mama's side, too? Knowing that?"

His father's eyes moved and looked at him. There was a different look in them now.

Why had he asked it?

His father looked down, and when he looked up again, the look was gone, and there was no anger in his eyes. But then his father spoke, and a little of what had been in his eyes was in his voice.

"It ain't much," he said. "What I can tell you 'bout her side, even 'bout her 'fore I met her in Bennington. All that went with her, and there ain't no way to get it back now. Just like I... We. Just like we can't never get her back." He took the pipe from his mouth and rested his arm on his knee. "Emma might be able to tell some. Probably quite a lot. Just remember, though, whatever she tells you 'bout your mother's side is her view and that she's your aunt; she ain't your mother. It's just like I was telling you earlier, 'bout your gran' pa and how it would be better if it was him telling you the things that I'll be telling you tonight. All right, then," he said, puffing on the pipe, his voice growing livelier. "Like I was saying.

You was too little to remember your gran' pa. You'll know him, though, by the time I'm through teaching you 'bout all the things he tole and taught me. It'll be just like the two of you have been sitting here all your eight years. Damn this pipe."

"Seven years, Pa. I won't be eight till March."

"Seven, eight, don't make no nevermind," he said, puffing and talking at the same time. "What matters is that you understand what it is I'm telling you. There," he said, having succeeded in sucking life into the pipe once more. Then he smiled. He had the pipe stem clamped between his teeth, and the skin was creased around his mouth and eyes. His teeth were tinted yellow by the firelight.

He did not smile back at his father. Just then he heard the wind again, the sound blowing deep and low out of nowhere, and he felt a coldness run up his arms and back that made him shudder.

"Now I'll tell you the other thing your gran' pa said." He sucked, then blew the smoke up past his nose. "He said that after knowing where you come from, the only other thing worth knowing is who you are; what you are. And why. Where you come from is just part of who you are. But the who and the what and the why's the most important. You learn that and you'll've learned as much as there is to know on this earth. Probably not one in ten people ever do it, though."

"And you'll teach me that, too?"

His father leaned forward.

"Nope. Can't. Something you gotta learn on your own just like everyone else. Those that learn it, anyway. But that's why your gran' pa brung me here. He tole me that there weren't no better place to find all that out than right here, in these woods."

"By myself! You don't mean tonight!"

"Easy, boy." His father's eyes fixed on him. "You still scared of it, ain'cha?"

He swallowed, and he could feel his Adams apple move in his throat. He nodded.

"Figured as much. Two years, but you still carting it around. You scared of it now?"

He shook his head. "Just a little, maybe."

"How come?"

He looked at the fire, then back at his father. "'Cause you're here, I guess."

He heard the pipe rap against the log. Then his father blew through it and rapped it again.

"God damn," his father said, enunciating each word. Then he looked at him. "Well, relax. Ain't nothing gonna happen tonight. But you can't cart that scaredness around with you forever. I'll see to that, and one day I'll show you how to get rid of it."

"How?"

"Never mind that for now. It's a long ways off. For you it'll be part of it. Part of finding out the who you are and the what you are or you won't never be rid of it." He pushed the pipe into his coat pocket.

"When, though? When will that be?" There was no hardness in his father's face, so he knew it was okay to ask.

"Can't say. Won't be tomorrow. Won't even be this year, or next. You'll know it when it happens, though, if it happens. And I intend to see that you get the chance. For you, it'll be in these woods. That I'm sure of. Has to be, 'cause these woods is the one thing on god's earth that you the most ascared of."

For a moment their eyes met and held each other. Then he turned his eyes away.

Except for maybe you, he said to himself, looking into the crackling fire.

Then his father coughed.

"There's one other thing your gran' pa told me," he said. "It's about these woods. He said... and these are his words... best as I can remember them. He said: the souls of all who have ever lived dwell in the woods. And you and me? We ain't nothing but intruders here, come to learn the truths that only the dead can tell. I hear their voices in the wind through the leaves in the night, in the rush of clear-running streams in the dawn's mist. Speaking to me... To you... To any that comes here. But one's gotta devote a lifetime of hard listening—of learning to listen with the heart—to ever hope of decipherin' the truths from those wandering souls.

"Anyway, them's his words. A bit fancier than I could ever say, but there was another side to your gran' pa. A bookish side... kinda like you. But I remembered the words and just tole them to you best as I could remember.

"There'll be times when you feel them souls, like I do. I feel them all the time when I'm in these woods. 'Specially when I'm alone. I hear their voices, too. Hollows you out. Makes you feel...

well, kinda humble, I guess. Kinda like you're amongst something bigger than you, greater than you. I guess maybe it's like for some folks when they go to church. There's some of them that feel God there, in church I mean, and it makes them feel different than any other place on this earth. This is my church. And I've learned to listen to the voices. And now I know where it is I come from, and who I am, what I am, and why. Some day... I hope some day... You'll know that, too. Some day, these woods will talk to you."

Once before, he had remembered that night, but so very long ago. Like everything else, he'd locked it away. So he wouldn't have to think about it, or remember. God. He'd known the truth all along. It shouldn't have surprised him that his old man would dump him out in the middle of nowhere five years after that night. He'd as much as told him he was going to. He'd put that night out of his mind. And he knew why now. God, he knew.

The pain poured out of him. It seemed to fill and empty him at the same time as he thought about the night he had forced himself to forget.

Who you are, what you are, and why. His old man had been right. He'd learned those things here, in these woods. He was a liar. He'd turned his whole life into a lie. He wasn't what his old man made him but what he made himself. And he knew why, why he'd convinced himself his old man tried to kill him, not sure now whether he actually believed that on the day he walked out of those woods whole again, or only long after, not until after his old man died. He had even convinced himself that he hated his old man. And he'd done all those things for one reason. Because he had to. He had to in order to go on living with himself and what he'd done to his old man on the day he died.

December 1925

They had waited more than an hour and not seen a deer. He was huddled in a blow-down and had not moved. He kept searching the dead forest with his eyes. Yet every few minutes his eyes were drawn to Dick.

Dick was ten yards away, hiding behind a mound of bushes and boulders. During the last hour, he moved constantly. First his head popped out from behind the rocks. Later, just the rifle barrel. Later still, all of him so he could see the red and black hunter's plaid of Dick's coat and the bright red hat, ear flaps tied up, that was at least three sizes too small and sat atop his head like a cardinal trying to hatch a coconut.

Just then Dick stood again. He came from behind the boulders and climbed onto one of the smaller rocks and, leaning forward, peeped through the bushes. He could see that Dick had the pistol stuck down the front of his trousers again, the pistol he had brought for, of all things, rabid squirrels. Dick was always latching onto something, and this was the latest. Suddenly the woods were full of squirrels foaming at the mouth. Squirrels didn't get rabies, but try telling that to Dick.

He watched Dick fidget on the rock. Then he saw his right foot slip off. Dick jerked it back and tried to plant it, but it was too late. Farther and farther forward he leaned, and then too far. His right arm, holding the rifle, shot out straight while his left arm began to circle wildly, and the next thing, Dick was falling into the bush amid a thundering: "awww-awww-awww-awww shi-i-i-i-i-i-t!"

He closed his eyes and shook his head. When he opened them, Dick was still face down in the bush, struggling to free himself.

"Davy. Davy," he yelled. "Crisesake, give me a hand!"

What was the use? They wouldn't see a bird now, let alone a deer.

He watched a few seconds before leaving his cover. Dick was still trying to free himself.

"For god's sake, Dick, you can make more noise than a zoo full of horny chimpanzees. Quit thrashin' and get up."

"I can't get up, yah goddamn idiot. Give me a hand."

"You are a sight. You look like a whale beached on a biscuit of shredded wheat." He laughed.

"Goddamn it, Davy. If you don't give me a hand, when I get out of this thing, I'm gonna blow your ass off."

"Now, now. No need to get testy. Why not just accept you're top heavy and can't tie your shoes without fallin' on your head?"

"Are you gonna help me or not!"

"Al-l-l-l right. Sure do wish I had a camera, though. I'd like to save your posterior for posterity."

"When I get free, I'm gonna pepper your posterior with buckshot."

Laughing, he laid his rifle down and was about to extend his hand when Dick gave a mighty wrench. With that, Dick's rifle broke free and out he came, rolling side over side, but he stopped fast when he hit the ground. When he did, he was looking straight down the barrels of Dick's shotgun.

" Dick!" he yelled, dropping to the ground.

Then Dick was on his feet, the visor of the red hat pointing over his left ear.

He looked at Dick from the ground. Dick looked enormous, a slab of concrete dressed in hunter's clothes.

"You are a piece of work," he said, getting to his feet.

"You talkin' to me?" Dick turned and looked behind himself. He watched as Dick's rifle swung and pointed straight at him again.

"Jesus christ! Put that gun down before you kill somebody."

"Uh, sorry. No need to worry, though. The safety's on. See?"

 Dick raised the double-barreled shotgun and squeezed one trigger. There was a roar as the gun discharged.

"Jesus fucking christ! What the hell is wrong with you?"

"What? What's the matter?"

"You're like hunting with a big kid. What were you doing there—hunting, or trying to teach yourself to fly?"

"Lost my balance is all. Minor infraction. The safety musta come off when I was stuck in that bush."

"Why were you standing in the first place? You're supposed to stay still when you're hunting, not go thrashin' around."

"Aw, com'on, Davy. I couldn't see nothin' behind that bush. Seemed to me that if I couldn't see, I couldn't shoot. Answer? Move. So I did. It was all very logical. At most, only a minor infraction to the HCGP."

"The what? What's this infraction nonsense?"

"The HCGP? Hunter's Code of Good Practices. For certain you've heard of the HCGP, great outdoorsman that you are."

"No, I haven't. It's just another one of the goddamn dumb things you made up."

"Forgive me," Dick said, "but I gotta piss so bad I swear I heard my kidneys float past my ears two hours ago, and they had oars. You just wait here and go on bein' mad and beautiful and I'll be back."

Dick batted his eyes, then tiptoed away.

"Wait! For crisesake."

Dick turned. "Aw, come on, Davy, what now?"

He put out his hand, level with Dick's groin. "The pistol. Give me the goddamn thing before you blow your balls off."

"Here." Dick pulled the pistol from his trousers and clapped it into his open hand. The pistol discharged, the bullet ricocheting off the nearby rocks.

"Son of a bitch!" But the sound had not even died when Dick thundered toward the bushes. He ran bent over and holding himself between the legs. When he reached the cover of the bushes, he straightened.

Shaking his head, he sat on a rock and waited for Dick. And waited. It seemed a full five minutes, and Dick was still in the bushes. Dick was looking at the sky and groaning.

"What the hell did you have for breakfast—a beer keg?"

Dick waved for him to be quiet.

"Well hurry it up. And do you have to make so much noise? You're supposed to be hunting, not grunting."

"Can't hurry this!" Dick said without turning, his voice booming. "This is life's second greatest pleasure."

He was quiet a moment. "Oh yeah. What's the first?"

"Been reserving judgment on that," Dick called back. "I'll tell yah, though. I'll be powerful disappointed if there don't turn out to be nothing better than taking a piss. That'd really suck."

"You know what? You're Mr. Excitement. Maybe we could get together Saturday night and do something thrilling, like... I don't know— Like melt down those bean cans and build us a new truck— one that farts!"

Dick came out of the bushes, zipping his trousers. He smiled down at him.

He smiled back. "Straighten out your hat. Or is it your head that's on crooked?"

"You through being sore?"

"Yeah, I'm through. Wasn't really sore, anyway."

Dick straightened his hat. "Whiskey," he said.

He looked right, then back at Dick. "Whiskey what?"

"Well, good whiskey, maybe. Heard good whiskey used to be quite the thing. Not that rotgut Sutter makes back at the camp."

"You do talk in riddles," he said. "What on god's earth are you babbling about now!"

"I thought we were talking about whiskey. What were you talking about?" Dick looked confounded.

"Don't start. I'm warning you. I've got a loaded gun and I know how to use it. Now, slowly, put your mind in gear." Then he shouted: "What about the goddamn whiskey!"

"Wish you'd stick to one level. One minute I can hardly hear you, and the next you're shouting the bark off trees. Bad habit. Might cost a loved one his hearing one day."

"Dick!" Everything stopped and it was utterly quiet. "You have got to be the most aggravating, infuriating, exasperating goddamndest human being ever put on the face of god's green earth."

Dick just looked at him. "You think that 'cause of your limited connections. Anyway, the whiskey. Was thinking it might be number one was all. You know, life greatest pleasure?"

"Why couldn't you have just come out and said that? No, you've got to put me through five minutes of torture. Anyway, you're wrong. You drink too much of anything, even the good stuff, and it blows your head up. Hey, maybe that's what happened to your head. Tell me, did that hat fit when you bought it?"

"Didn't buy it. Just borrowed. Makes me look official, don't it? Meets all the specifications set down in the HCGP."

He eyed Dick, evaluating the effect of the hat. "You may look like a lot of things, but you can rule out official."

"Petty jealousy. According to the HCGP, a hat like this might keep some fool from shooting me accidentally."

"From what I've seen, the only fool likely to shoot you is you yourself... or me. And if I do it, it won't be any accident."

"Is that a fact. Well, come on then, and I'll show you what hunting is all about."

"Seriously? We're lucky if there's a deer left Vermont."

"Well, it ain't my fault if you made a ruckus, yelling and screaming at me, and scared 'em all off."

"Me! Why you goddamn turnip. They probably cleared out as soon as they caught wind of you. What is that odor?"

"Oil of citronella."

"For what?"

"Disguise my odor."

"And where did you... No, let me guess." There was a knowing pause. Then they said the initials together: "H-C-G-P."

"Dick," he said, "normally any time you want to disguise your odor, I'm all for it. But citronella? That's bug repellant. There aren't any goddamn bugs this time of year. You know what? You're a one-man, half-brained, walking block of deer repellant. God you stink."

Dick smelled underneath his arm. Then he raised his head and, with his eyes closed, assumed an expression as if he had just been transported to paradise.

"Wonderful stuff," he said. "Might even start using it as aftershave. Attract the women like flies."

"Flies are about the only thing you're going to attract."

"Sex," Dick said.

"What?"

"Sex."

"What, with you? No thanks."

"Wasn't no proposition. God, you dumber than a bag of hammers. Just occurred to me that might be number one. Don't know about you, but I'd sure like to find out. You?"

He looked off into the trees, then at the sky. "What's say we start to head back," he said. "Don't like the look of that sky." He turned and started walking.

"Hey, come on now, Davy boy. What is it?"

He shook his head. "Nothing. Just think we should start."

"Seems like a man ought to be able to talk about something like that with his best friend. Course, if you don't want to, we don't have to. Course, you'd think you'd be able—"

"Dick!"

"Then again, what are friends for except to ignore. You know the old saying: A friend in need is a pain in the ass. Must make a note to get those included in the HCGP."

He was still walking away from Dick when he stopped and exhaled. Then he turned. "Look. Maybe some time we'll talk about it. But not now."

Dick held him with his eyes. Then he looked away. "Sure. Sure thing, Davy. We'll talk about it sometime."

"Look, why don't we start back?" he said, trying to put some animation in his voice. "Looks like a storm is going to break. We can slow hunt as we go along and try to get part of the way back before it hits."

"Okay by me."

"You ever slow hunted?"

"Hell, this is only my third time hunting, but I can't imagine nothin' slower than this."

He closed his eyes. "Never mind. Just watch me and do what I do. This being only your third time, if we see a deer, it's yours, okay? And no talking."

He swung his pack onto his back, and each of them retrieved his rifle.

For a time, they proceeded at a walking pace but, when they had gone far enough to be in an area that had not been disquieted by their shooting and shouting, he restrained Dick with his hand and slowed the pace to half. Later, he did it again.

From that point, they moved slowly, stopping for a half minute or longer after a few steps to search the woods before they took a few more steps and stopped again.

It was a long time later that he saw the buck.

He touched Dick, and the two of them froze and watched the buck descend a hill and walk out onto the level ground about thirty yards in front of them.

He knew that it had probably started feeding at dawn and was heading back to where it bedded. It would stay there until dusk, and then it would feed again.

The buck had not seen or smelled them because it continued, unhurried, to cross the path in front of them.

Out of the corner of his eye, he saw Dick's rifle go up. But then the buck either caught the movement or their scent. For an instant, it looked at them. Already he was saying under his breath: "Shoot! Shoot!" And just as the buck constricted for the first springing leap that would carry it into the trees and to safety, he heard Dick's gun discharge and saw the shot explode into a pine tree about twelve feet above where the buck was standing. The shot blew off bark in a shower of fragments.

The buck was gone before he felt his butt hit the ground, the laughter already shaking him. He fell over, pointing first at Dick, then at the tree, drawing his legs up to his midsection.

Dick stood over him. "Appears I missed."

And that started him on a new fit. "Missed? Oh, god... I'll say... 'Less... 'Less there was a buck hiding in that tree that I didn't see."

He rolled on his back and laughed until it hurt. Then, he took a deep breath and let it out in a noisy hoot. He pushed himself up on one arm.

"God, you really are a piece of work. Who in hell taught you to shoot?"

"No one. Just come to me natural I guess. Ah hell, Davy, I know it ain't obvious, but truth is, I don't know the first thing about shooting. Well, what in hell is so funny about that?" Dick asked, for he had started to laugh again. "So I don't know how to shoot. No reason to go mocking a fella."

"It's nothing," he said, holding up his hand. "Only I just got this vision. You... You're standing right where you are, see? Your gun loaded and ready. And then, two or three hundred deer come out of the woods down there and start walking toward you. This big, enormous herd with a huge buck in the lead. So you... You raise your gun and start blasting away. Damn, there's shot flying all over hell and creation. Trees are dropping, bushes are blasted stripped of leaves, birds lose their feathers in terror, but do those deer bolt? Nope, they just keep on coming, and when they're about five feet in front of you, you run out of shells. And then the big lead buck turns to the others and says, "You see. I told you the safest place was right in front of him."

He gave out a whoop and, rising, clapped Dick on the shoulder, and, after watching him a moment, the mock seriousness melted from Dick's face and he laughed, too.

It was Dick who finally spoke. "Now what?" he asked. "You wanna do it some more?"

"No, no," he said. "I've had all I can take for one day.

Let's just head back. The trees need a break. They aren't safe as long as you're in the woods."

"Okay," Dick said. "I don't think I could really shoot nothing anyway."

"I know," he said, the tone of amusement gone from his voice. "I knew not even you could miss a buck by that much unless you did it on purpose," and he patted Dick on the shoulder.

They were just getting ready to start when he felt the first raindrop on his hand. The gray sky was spread like a blanket above the bare trees.

"We best get moving," he said. "Looks like this one could last awhile. Better put on your poncho."

"I didn't bring it," Dick said.

"What do you mean you didn't bring it? I told you to stuff it in my pack."

"I know. I just figured if it did anything, it would snow. So I left it. And don't get yourself set to give me no lecture, Mister Mom. I didn't bring it and that's all there is to it."

He took his pack off and pulled from it a drab-colored poncho. "Here," he said offering it to Dick. "Wear mine."

"No. I ain't gonna take yours. It was my mistake. I should be the one to do without."

"Suit yourself." He put his pack on and slipped the poncho over his head. He covered his head with the hood.

"Okay, let's walk. Maybe we can make some distance before it opens up."

They walked briskly, but the rain gradually intensified. Then the wind rose, and the rain fell harder. It was not a driving rain, but it was steady and cold. It was very cold rain.

"Can't we stop and hole up?" Dick asked about a half-hour later. "I'm plum chilled." Dick's clothes were water-laden. He was shivering, and there were puddles around him on the ground.

"Where?" he answered. "There's no shelter around here that I know of, and a fire out in the open, if we could get one lit, isn't going to help you. The best thing is to get back to camp as quick as we can. You all right?"

"Sure. I'm all right. Wish I could stop this damn shivering though. Ain't never felt rain this cold."

They went on, maintaining a pace just short of having to break stride and trot. The rain continued to fall, steady and cold and angled just slightly by the wind so that the tree trunks were stained darker on the facing side

They walked for maybe another half-hour when he heard Dick call out: "Davy!" His voice was panicked. When he turned, Dick was on his knees, supporting himself on straight arms, and he was looking at the ground. Even from where he stood, he could see Dick shaking.

He ran to him.

"Dick!"

Dick raised his head. "I-I-I-I-It's my legs. Davy... I-I-I-I can't move m-m-my legs s-s-s-so good. What's happening?"

"Don't worry. Can you get up? Come on, try. I'll carry you. It's only another half-mile."

There was no answer but, when he saw Dick struggling to stand, he threw down his rifle and hastened to get his shoulder under Dick's midsection. A second later, he felt Dick's full weight come down on him, and he strained to right himself and pull his feet together. The weight was awesome, and Dick was shivering so fiercely, he was afraid it was going to knock him off balance, but he straightened and was able to hold him.

He'd never make it. Not a half-mile carrying two-hundred-and-fifty pounds.

"Hang on," he said to Dick. "I'll get you out. Talk to me."

"I'm t-t-too c-c-c-cold," Dick said.

"Goddamn it, I said talk to me!"

"W-w-why?"

"Don't argue. You don't need to know, you dumb son of a bitch! Talk! I don't care what you talk about, but talk! And you keep talking, you hear!"

Dick started talking. His words were slurred and the shivering made him chatter.

Good god, he had it bad. He knew the progression. The shivering would go on for awhile. Then it would suddenly stop, and Dick would feel warm. After that, it was one of two things. Either Dick would pass out, or, more likely, he would start to hallucinate. His old man had been the first to tell him that, and then he'd seen it once—a man so cold he could barely move, and God only knew what kinds of things he was seeing in his head. There was no telling how long the hallucinations would last. But eventually he'd pass out. The end wasn't far beyond that. By then, there might not be anything he could do to save him.

He wasn't about to let that happen.

For awhile, he listened to Dick babble, but then he merely kept himself aware of Dick's voice and listened for any change. Now he concentrated on his walking, on trying to maintain the same rapid pace as before.

For a time, he was nearly able to do that, but the pain in his knees and back from Dick's bulk was growing worse by the minute. Dick was so heavy it felt like his shoulder would be torn from his body.

After covering what he guessed was about a quarter of a mile, he spoke. " Dick. I gotta rest. Just a few minutes. I'm going to lean you... against a boulder. Try to keep... yourself from sliding."

He lowered Dick as gently as he could and reclined his lifeless form against a large boulder. Dick started to slide. He caught him and pressed his body hard against Dick's. His shoulder felt light now and floating away from his body.

"Start talking... again," he said to Dick between gulped breaths. "Let me hear... that beautiful voice. I just need... to gather myself. That's all."

The raindrops were collecting in pools on the boulder and then running in rivulets down the sides. Dick was sodden. His red cap had fallen off. Now his black hair was wet and stringy and lay close against his head.

"I'm sorry, Davy. Stupid… about the poncho." Dick's voice sounded full of a great weariness.

"Don't worry about that now. Just try to hold on."

"Doan need to hurry," Dick said flatly. "Ain't cold no mo'. Jus' feel so sleepy now."

"Don't sleep! Try to keep on talking."

"Can't. All talk' out."

Dick's eyes were vacant and heavy lidded.

He shook him. " Dick!" He struck him flat-handed across the face, but Dick did not rouse.

"Come on, Dick, come on. Don't go out on me." He leaned into Dick's midsection and hoisted him on his shoulder again. Dick felt even heavier now, and the pain returned immediately to his knees. His thighs felt rubbery under the weight.

Another ten minutes. Fifteen maybe. He had to do it.

He walked as fast as his fatigue would allow, without stopping to jostle Dick or to rebalance his dead weight on his shoulder. He did those things on the move.

Then there was the smell of smoke in the damp air. He kept his eyes straight ahead, looking for the squat brown buildings of the logging camp. But the trees went on and on.

He started to fix on a tree and count the steps to it—forty-five, forty-six, forty-seven—and then to another. He was trying to keep his mind off the weight.

Shit, where the hell was that fucking camp? Please, god, please don't let it be too late.

Dick had long since stopped making any sound. He was simply limp and sodden and tremendously heavy.

He was nearly at the brink of collapse when he saw the end of the trail and, beyond, the brown parallel logs of the camp mess and the roof of the porch that ran the full length of the building. Smoke blew from the chimney straight toward the ground.

There was someone on the porch, stooped over, but from the red shirt, he knew it must be Sutter.

A few seconds later, he entered the open ground of the camp. "Sutter!" he shouted.

The figure straightened and turned. It was Sutter, arms full of firewood. Sutter let the wood fall to the porch. He ran down the steps and charged across the open ground, ignoring the puddles and mud.

"Help me with him!" he said to Sutter.

He set Dick's feet on the ground and Sutter grabbed him under the arms. He took Dick's legs.

"What's the matter with him? He shot?" Sutter asked as they started toward the building.

"No. Exposure. Get him inside fast."

"He still alive?"

"How the christ do I know! Just move!"

Sutter had left the door unlatched. He kicked it open now, and they carried Dick inside.

"Put him on the floor near the stove," he ordered Sutter.

By the stove, he knelt and felt the side of Dick's neck.

"There's a pulse, but it's not good," he told Sutter. Sutter was bent over, watching, his hands on his knees. "Get some blankets while I get his clothes off. And then we gotta get something into him to get his temperature up."

"Got some moonshine. That'll —"

"No. Coffee. Even water. Long as it's hot. But not too hot."

"Always got coffee," Sutter said. "I'll get some."

In a minute, Sutter was back with a mug of steaming coffee. While Sutter was gone, he had removed Dick's wet jacket and shirt. His skin was white and bloodless.

"Put the coffee down and help me get his boots and pants off."

Sutter put the mug on the floor, out of the way, and each began to work on one of Dick's boots. Sutter got his off first.

"Here. Let me," Sutter said to him. "Your hands are too cold to work and you look nearly spent."

"I'll get the blankets then. Where are they?"

"No blankets here. Just some old tablecloths. In the kitchen. On the shelf in the closet."

He ran to the kitchen and grabbed a half-dozen of the folded cloths from the shelf. By the time he returned, Sutter had the other boot off and was working on Dick's trousers.

"Jesus," Sutter said. "Never seen a man such an awful color before. Like putty."

He dropped all but one of the cloths and, opening it, draped it over the wood stove to warm it. "Can you prop him up?" he asked Sutter as he tended to the cloth.

Sutter lifted Dick's torso. "Goddamn, he's a heavy one. How far'd you have to carry him?"

"I don't know. Far enough. Hold him up there now."

He wrapped Dick's upper body in the warm tablecloth.

"Should I try to get the coffee into him long as we got him upright?" Sutter asked.

"No. Won't be able to. He's got to come around a little before we can do that. Let's get the fire built up."

They eased Dick to the floor and, while Sutter went to the porch to fetch firewood, he warmed another tablecloth and wrapped Dick's legs in it. One by one, he warmed the other tablecloths and covered Dick with them.

Sutter returned with an armful of wood. "Shouldn't we rub

his arms and legs to get the circulation going?" he asked, feeding the stove.

"No Best to take it slow. Try to get him warm inside and out."

"You look almost as bad as him. Why don't you go rest?"

"No. I've got to stay with him till he's out of this. I'm okay. You got more coffee?"

"Sure," Sutter answered.

"I'll drink this one then, as long as we can't get it into him. Can you help me get this poncho off? I'm starting to melt." He could feel the sweat running under his arms.

Sutter helped remove the poncho. Then he let his pack slip to the floor and sat by Dick and drank the coffee, feeling its warmth slide down to his stomach. The heat by the stove was growing oppressive.

He felt of Dick's neck again, and it seemed the pulse was stronger, or was he only imagining it? But just as he finished his coffee, Dick moaned.

"He's coming, Sutter," he said excitedly. "You see that? He's coming. Get me some fresh coffee, quick. And put a little cold water in it so it's not too hot."

Sutter took the mug and left to fill it. When he returned, Dick was groaning softly, but he was not conscious.

"Try to make him drink," he said to Sutter. "But real slow. Don't burn his mouth."

"Shouldn't burn him," Sutter answered. "Put cold water in like you said. Still good and warm, but it ain't boiling."

"Good."

Sutter put the mug to Dick's lips and tilted it and put one hand under Dick's chin. He raised Dick's head slightly. Then Dick coughed.

"What's happening?" he asked Sutter.

"'Pears to be going down. He ain't come to, though."

"That's all right. Keep it going into him slow and steady."

Several minutes later Sutter looked at him and said, "he's almost finished it. Should I get some—" But he stopped. "Hey. His eyelids are moving."

He felt Dick's body tense in his arms and shudder. He eased him to the floor. Dick's eyes were half open, but he was still far away.

Sutter got another mug of coffee, and they got that into him. Then he sat on the floor, Dick lying between him and the stove. He stared at the stove, not wishing to talk with Sutter. The minutes went by.

"Davy? That you?" Dick's voice was weak. His eyes were open, and he held his head a little off the floor and looked at him down his nose. He shivered.

"Yeah, it's me. Who's asking?"

"We back at camp?"

"That's right."

"I don't remember. You carry me?"

"Yeah, I carried you."

"Shoulda left me. Stupid. 'Bout the poncho. Why didn't yah just leave me?

He smiled and turned his head away and looked at the stove. "'Because of the trees. Knew they wouldn't be safe long as you were in the woods."

He looked back at Dick. Dick smiled weakly and put his head on the floor. Both were quiet.

Then Dick said, "Davy?"

"Yeah."

"Know what's number one?"

"No. What?"

"Being alive," Dick said. "Just being alive."

9

He heard a rustling high up and behind him. Then raucous cawing shattered the brittle silence.

Laughing?

He looked at the pines on the nearby knoll, his head careening as he turned.

The cawing stopped off, then started again. He caught movement near the tops of the pines. The crows were two silhouettes, wings outspread and then folding against their bodies, and then the black wedges of their beaks opened against the sky and their bodies coughed the awful sound into the solitude: "Caw-caw-caw-caw-caw."

What was the matter with him? Just crows. Two crows quarreling over a branch.

He rested his head on his arm, which was draped over the granite rock.

They'd be quarreling over him soon, wouldn't they?

Christ, there was a thought. The hard black beaks pecking at him. Pecking out his eyes. Pecking to get at the soft parts.

"Shut up! Shut up!" he hollered, rising from the rock.

The black birds flapped and swayed on their perches. He could feel their black eyes watching him. He rested his head again and looked into the fire.

Without rising, he stirred the embers and repositioned the wood to burn hotter. Then he fed the fire. He rested his head again and looked at the smashed compass a few inches away on the rock.

Look what he'd done... not just to the compass, but to his life.

For twenty years. Longer.

And his old man. What of him? Is it possible his old man had loved him? He remembered that last look in his eyes. Oh god, if it was true, why did that have to be the last thing his father was to know? The last act of a loving son. He might as well have kicked him into Hell.

He looked at the compass, cold and gray against the gray rock, the stag's head dented and deformed from the bashing.

No, it couldn't be. There were too many things that said it couldn't be true.

What difference did it make? He couldn't take it back any more than he could fix that compass. Was there any wonder he'd sensed his old man in that hunk of metal all these years? That he could barely abide the touch of it? Did he sense him in there now? Or in these woods? Or had he smashed that out of existence, too?

He looked at the compass, stared at it, his heritage, his birthright—smashed, violated, so long abhorred but abhorred no longer. That was true, wasn't it? There was something emerging inside, not there yet, but embryonic, an impulse to accept the compass as his right.

His heart calmed, and the anguish within him unknotted.

"Pa, if you can hear me," he said, "I'm sorry. So so sorry."

He listened, but beneath the dark sky there was only the infinite, yawning silence of the valley flowing into him, as if he were its very object. Even the crows were silent, eyeing him curiously from their lofty perch.

Well, Pa, he said to himself, I can't undo it… can't take it back. But somehow… maybe there's a way I can make it up. By not letting you down this time. By not giving up.

He made a tight fist.

He'd try. He'd show him it hadn't been for nothing.

He closed his eyes.

Funny to think about it now, that day when he was twelve. The thing that his old man wanted to happen had happened. He'd shown him how to stop being afraid of the woods. How had he gotten everything so messed up? Was that all his fault?

More cawing spewed from the trees. He looked up just as one crow, wings flapping, leapt from its perch and sank earthward, the slow thrusts of its wings raising it again in jerks and bobs. It circled, rising above the trees, and finally lit at the top of the pine adjacent to the one it had left. It cawed defiantly at the other crow.

Filthy black bastards. How long would he have to listen to that?

On the ground near the fire was a walnut-sized stone. He closed his hand on it and pushed clear of his granite pillow. His head circled unsteadily. And then his stomach circled after it. He let the stone fall from his hand, and he laid flat on the ground and held his eyes closed until the queasiness passed. All the while, the crows kept cawing.

He had to get out of there. He couldn't stand them waiting like that. Where was the splint? He wasn't going to give up. Not yet.

He got onto his stomach, but his arms were too rubbery and heavy to pull him forward, and the fire in his leg rose to a scalding pitch with his movements.

Grimacing, he stopped.

Who was he kidding? He wasn't going anywhere.

He looked at the crows and narrowed his eyes.

Maybe he could at least get the splint back on. That way he'd be ready when his strength came back. It was just that the sickness had taken so much out of him. In awhile he'd be all right again; he'd see.

He set himself and willed his arms to pull his body forward. He retrieved the splint, then worked himself into a sitting position, his back supported by the granite rock.

With his head turned away and his lungs full and locked, he dragged his leg up to him and pulled his trouser leg down. The pain ate at him as he positioned the splint and tied it.

He didn't have to worry about tying it too tight. The leg was rotting anyway. But the bone could work its way through even more, and he might still bleed. He couldn't chance that.

When the crows cawed again, the harshness of their voices ran through him like barbed wire being pulled through his veins, and he went rigid until it stopped.

They'd drive him crazy if he didn't get out of there. Them and the leg and the cold. Why couldn't he warm up?

He fed several pieces of wood to the fire and, using a stick, moved them to catch the draft. The fire popped, spitting out a shower of sparks. One glowing fragment landed on his right hand, burning him even though he was quick to bat it off.

"Jesus fucking christ," he said. Didn't he have enough to deal with without another goddamn pain?

He rubbed the burn with his finger and licked it. Then he eased back against the rock and, looking into the fire, sucked at the burn, trying to kill the sting...

"What is it?" she said.

He glanced at her over his shoulder before turning back to the fire.

"Jussa spar'," he said, not taking his hand from his mouth. "Caugh' my han'."

He saw her in his mind now. He could see her any time he wanted. She was sitting on the log, watching him, elbows on her knees and her chin resting on the bridge her arms formed between. Her hair was pulled back and tied and trailed onto her back, and she was wearing a blue wool shirt and beige wide-wale corduroys. But what he could see clearest were her eyes, the eyes that too many times in the past four weeks had looked flat and dead. Before then, before Wilkey, her eyes had been shining and depthless. They were the windows through which he could see all things, of this world and beyond. If he had one wish, it would be to revive the life he had seen in her eyes and then to make her eyes shine for him. Could she even begin to understand how much he loved her?

He was sitting on his heels, looking into the fire. The embers were breathing with the morning currents, with a glow that swelled and ebbed in contrast to the frantic crackling of the flames.

He squeezed his eyes shut. Then he heard her move, and he tensed. But if she had stood, she did not come closer.

After taking a deep breath, he wiped his eyes with his hands and, fixing his composure, stood and turned to her.

"Why bother with this then? With coming here?"

She had stood, and now she had her hands in her pockets, flat against her buttocks.

"Because this is important to you. I wanted to try to understand this part of you."

"This isn't important to me. You are."

"Isn't it?"

"No. I'd give it up in a minute. For you I would."

"David, you're kidding yourself. You couldn't stay away if you wanted to. You don't even know why, do you?"

"I don't know what you mean."

"Don't you... or do you really not know yourself at all?" She looked at him entreatingly. "David, you're looking for something here, don't you realize that? I don't know what. Maybe it's yourself. Or maybe something else. But I'd like to understand... if you'll let me."

"And that's why you're going away? To understand?"

"No, of course not. Don't talk nonsense."

"You think by spending one day in the woods you'll understand this part of me?"

"David, please, I'm trying. What more do you want from me?" She exhaled deeply. "David, I have to make this trip. Please just accept that and trust me."

"I do trust you, and I'm trying to understand, but I just don't understand why you have to go away to... to... to search your soul or whatever it is you want to call it."

"There's more to it than that."

"What more?"

"It's not something I can talk about. Not now. David, don't you understand that nothing is possible between us with me like I am right now?"

He bit the inside of his bottom lip and let his eyes close before he looked at her again. "I do understand. Only don't abandon me, Carrie. Please."

She came to him then and took his hand and pressed it against her cheek. "I know," she said. "What it's like to love and not have the feeling returned. Who knows that better than I? I know you want to reach inside of me and wrench out a return of the feeling. But I also know that there is more pain in abandonment. I haven't abandoned you, David, believe me. But you have to give me this time. There's no hope of finding what you're looking for in me unless you do."

He nodded reluctantly.

"Dear David. I don't know whether you've acknowledged it to yourself, but you're suffering, and I can't help you. Maybe someday I'll be able to. When I come back." She stroked his cheek and looked at him tenderly.

"Can I ask you something?" he said.

"Certainly."

"Would you hold me? Just for a minute."

She looked into his eyes, then nodded.

They were the dead eyes. Weeks earlier he had finally told her that he was in love with her, but he knew it now. He would never make those eyes shine for him. Still, he could not bear to lose her.

She drew close to him, and he wrapped his arms around her and pulled her close. She reclined her head against him, and he stroked her hair and lifted her chin and kissed her on the forehead.

How at peace he felt. When she was that close, he could feel her come into him and calm the storm, and all the churning and surging stilled and became a deep, quiet pool.

"How I love you," he said. "I have never loved anyone, anything, the way I love you." He held her close. "Oh, Carrie. I used to think I couldn't love you any more than the way I did. But now, ever since I told you how I felt... I feel so empty, like nothing could ever hope to fill me."

"Shhhhh. Shhhh." she said below him.

"Just hold me a minute. I'm so at peace when you're in my arms. Nothing can touch me; nothing can hurt me."

"At least I can give you that," she said.

"I love you so much."

"It would be so much easier if you didn't."

"Carrie? Could I ask you something? Could I kiss you?"

"Do you think you should?"

"No, could I is what I asked?"

She was silent. Then she looked up at him.

"But of course."

He lowered his face to hers, and then his mouth was against hers, so sweet and warm. He held her close and pressed his lips to hers, kissing her long but gently. They broke, and kissed again, briefly, and then it was over. He drew her close.

"I'm sorry to have asked that of you, but it seemed... it only seemed right that a man at least ought to have kissed the woman he loves. But I'm sorry to have asked."

"It confused me. I felt some of your pain in your kiss, and it confused me."

"I didn't mean it to."

She looked up at him. "I've known," she said. "For a long time... not who it was, or what they did to you. But I've felt the hole in you. The emptiness. Whatever it is. I think I've sensed it in you for as long as I've known you."

He could feel her eyes probing his, and he could not bear it. He looked over her to the humped mountains of the Taconic Range.

"I want you to know that part of me wishes I could return the feeling. That part of me wishes I could fill the hole in you."

"If you loved me, it would be filled. You're the only one who could make me whole. I couldn't begin to tell anyone else how."

He looked back at the mountains.

Was that why she had responded to him these last few weeks, because part of her wished she could return the feeling? Or was he just a poor substitute for Wilkey, and she was just now realizing that he couldn't take his place in her life? It was the other part that was stronger. The part that couldn't return the feeling. The part that was taking her away.

He looked at her. "Come. Let's look at the valley."

He smiled and tried to brighten and took her hand. They walked out onto the rocky summit of the mountain and looked down to the Hoosic Valley. Below, the buildings were so small he could take in all of North Adams without turning his head. The valley opened to the south, their left, and in front of them were the rolling Taconics reaching to New York State and beyond. It was August, but some of the trees had already begun to turn the yellows and reds of the New England autumn.

"It's so lovely," she said. "What did you say the name of this mountain is?"

"Pine Cobble."

"How did you find this?"

"My father brought me here once. When I was a kid. Said it was a locale where the souls of the wilderness congregated, maybe because of the vistas. See that big one down there." He pointed left. "That's Mount Greylock. They say Melville could see it from his study in Pittsfield and that in wintertime, when it was covered with snow, it looked like the head of a white whale, and that's where he got the idea for Moby Dick." She was looking at him curiously. "But then, I guess no one reads Melville anymore, do they?"

"Melville?"

"I've always read a lot. Most of the time as a kid there wasn't anyone to play with. But you know all that."

"Yes. But good god… Melville? You're right. He's so tedious." She looked at the mountains again. "Your father was right, too," she said. "The view is beautiful."

"Yeah. He was right. About a lot of things."

They both were silent.

"Carrie," he said later without looking at her. "Please say you won't abandon me."

But she was silent, and then he knew she was not going to respond. Instead, she turned and went back to the fire.

July 1915

Perhaps he did not give himself to it consciously. But he did nothing to stop it, even after he recognized just how far the lying had gone. He could still remember the first big lie. His first year of school. He overheard a classmate tell his teacher that a horse bit him. And when he saw the reaction of the teacher, his classmates, he countered by saying loudly enough for the class to hear that a horse had once kicked him in the head. And then he showed them his scar. And there was an actual scar, but it was from when he tripped in the woods and bashed his head against the rock.

Over the years, he embellished the horse story. It had had such a wondrous effect. To it he added a metal plate implanted in his skull because of the severity of his trauma.

And later still, when the plate no longer seemed enough, he added two other horses to the original one—three stallions charging at his father across the pastureland of their farm. What was he do to? he asked. With his father's life in danger, he did the only thing he could, placed himself between his father and the onrushing horses. Two he managed to wave off, but it was the third, the biggest, that felled him. It reared and lashed out with its hoofs. For weeks after he laid unconscious in the hospital, his grateful father visiting every day and praying at his bedside. And on the day he finally opened his eyes, his father wept, the only time he ever saw his father cry.

And then there was the time some of his schoolmates belittled his father because his father was just a farmer, a man who worked the earth with his hands and was not the owner of a general store, or a banker, or a minister like their fathers. For that he created the Teddy Roosevelt lie, about how his father rode with the Rough Riders in Cuba and was a hero of the Spanish American War.

In fact, Mr. Roosevelt once dined at their little Vermont farmhouse. That was 1907. The president came unpublicized, escorted by four generals, to seek his father's counsel on a matter of military importance.

The president even stooped to shake his hand and asked if he were going to grow up to be a brave man like his father. And then his father told Mr. Roosevelt about the horses and how his son saved his life when only a boy of five.

And the president said, "bully," and then placed his hand on his shoulder and told him that the country needed men with such character and courage, and that he was sure he would grow up to be a great man someday.

For awhile the effect of these stories was marvelous. But over time, the lies became too outlandish, and his schoolmates began to think him queer. After that, even when he told the truth, people did not believe him or, at best, were skeptical. Even his one friend, Tim Merritt, stopped defending him and, later, stopped associating with him, too.

That was when it started. That was when he began to draw into himself. Slowly at first, but persistently, until he became a pitiable figure, solitary and withdrawn. People shrugged him off, said that he was off in another world. In fact, he became lost to another world. It was a world of his own creation, a world of fantasies and books. He read whenever he was not occupied with school, or doing chores, or making pilgrimages to the wilderness with his father.

He loved the world that reading revealed—by writers like Hawthorne, and Melville, and Twain. Especially Twain. But reading rendered him subject to wild imaginings. When he was fourteen, he actually fell in love with Becky Thatcher, spun his own fantasies about her—powerful fantasies in which he was always the hero, brave, superhuman in strength and in courage, saving her from certain death time after time—fantasies in which she loved him completely, perfectly, desperately.

But then, in his fifteenth year, reality smacked through the sheathing of his fantasy world, wounding him one last time before drawing the sheathing back around him. For in his fifteenth year, his father died, not alone and quietly, but with the audacity to die in front of him, provoking him to an act, so contemptible, that in time he utterly repressed it.

It was then that he began to lie to himself.

10

He felt more rested, yet a weakness languished in his arms and legs. For a long time, he had done nothing but feed the fire and watch the scud race up the valley beneath the gray clouds. The clouds were so low, only the bottom of the outcrop, his landmark, was visible above the tree tops.

He realized then that the crows had departed. They had gone silently, their absence conspicuous now only because of the absence of sound. Yet it was a disturbing silence, haunted by the memory of the raucous cawing and the black, piercing eyes.

They'd be back, he told himself. Gone to gorge themselves before the snow.

He looked at the pines where they had perched. He was half afraid he had overlooked them. But, no. The trees were empty.

Well, he didn't intend to be here when they returned.

Patting his chest, he located his watch and pushed it up under his shirt and pulled it out. He lowered himself to the ground and crawled into the open. Away from the fire, he noticed the smell of snow in the air. He looked at the outcrop. If it had been southwest when he started that morning, it must be roughly south now. He had to do it from memory; there was no shadow to help him.

It was west that he wanted to go. Wasn't that right? He couldn't remember.

He looked down the barrel of the valley. Except for several rolling mounds to the right, the valley floor was a sheet of granite for a hundred yards or so. Beyond, it was rocky and sparsely treed. At the far end, perhaps a half-mile, a mountain rose, obstructing a westerly course.

Satisfied that the valley ran roughly west, he dropped the lanyard over his head and warmed the watch in his hand before dropping it against his chest. Then he crawled to his fire, leaning close to draw in its warmth.

He felt stronger. Not strong, but enough to make another go at the crutch. The dizziness, slight, still lingered, and he could feel the approaching storm in his bones with a coldness that the fire was powerless to quell. He shuddered. Only his broken leg did not feel chilled. It was burning.

The snow would start soon. He'd seen it too many times to kid himself. The only question was how bad it would be. He'd better make some distance before he got the answer.

He retrieved the longer of the crutches and pulled himself onto his right foot, the pain roaring as his leg lifted free. In a minute, the pain found its level and, after scraping his father's note and the compass into his hand and putting them into his pocket, he hobbled westward.

He headed into the valley, the rolling mounds to his right. The next mound was not far, an eighth of a mile, maybe less. He'd try to make that before resting again.

With his right hand between the tines, under his arm, he was able to negotiate the rocky ground, but the going was difficult, inches at a time, and he could feel his strength draining each time he lifted his body. Soon his right foot was cramping. He put his weight on his heel to ease the constriction, then sat on a rock and worked the knot out.

He wished there was time to make another crutch. But he couldn't stop now. That would be a job for tonight, by the fire.

Then, far off, muffled by the distance or smothered in the dark, clouds, the harsh, diminutive voices of the crows reached his ears like the reoccurring chill from a bad dream. He held his breath. Then he heard the cawing stop, and he let his head tilt back and closed his eyes. When he opened them again, he was looking into the slate-gray sky, so low it seemed that he could touch it.

Was there any chance that it might rain? He'd have to find shelter to sit it out, but at least he'd be able to move again when it was over. He'd watched clouds all his life. But on a day like this, when it was close to freezing, there was just no way to tell whether it would snow or rain. Not even his old man could tell that.

He wriggled his toes and, satisfied that the cramp had passed, eased off the rock. As he stood, he spotted a tall bush. It was by the trees at the base of the knoll to his right. It appeared to be a high-bush blueberry. He hobbled to it. The bush was sparsely dotted with still-clinging berries, shriveled and almost black.

Resting his weight on the crutch, one by one he picked the berries and placed them in his left palm. When he had a dozen or so, he transferred them to his other hand and ate them. Even though they were dry, their sourness started the saliva running in his mouth again, but his stomach greeted the berries uneasily. He ate slowly, and, to his surprise, was able to keep the berries down. He ate until he had picked the bush nearly clean.

It felt so good to have wetness in his mouth again. And the sugar might help his strength. Funny to think what might save his life now, even a blueberry.

That was the right way to think, though. 'Eat,' his old man would say. 'Rest and eat. Don't stop to eat if you ain't tired. There's always something to eat, so don't worry.'

He peered down the valley.

He was tired. Damn tired. But he couldn't stop. He hoped he could reach the mountain before the snow started, before the light failed. Maybe he would recognize where he was then, or recognize something familiar, so that he could get his bearings. And then he could think about how he was going to make it through tomorrow.

For a long time, he pushed on steadily, the dizziness hovering in his head but not strong enough to steal his balance. He headed to a stand of birch. The trees were about fifty yards from the mound he sought. There, he sat and rested and stamped his foot against the reoccurring cramp.

He had done only a small fraction of a mile, he guessed. How much daylight was left? An hour?

He leaned on the birch and hung his head and exhaled and tried to catch his breath.

The first snowflake fell onto the rounded toe of his boot. He watched it, but it did not melt. Then he looked up into a fall of flakes drifting slow and silent.

So it wasn't going to hold off until he'd made camp for the night. Damn. Now he'd have to push himself.

He moved from under the trees and resumed his course. For a while, the snow fell with the same drifting lilt, the flakes landing silently and not melting, looking like little doilies against the green and black buffalo plaid of his shirt.

Soon, however, the flakes were falling faster and growing in size, and he knew the storm was coming into its own. The valley grew indistinct, the mountain at its end obliterated in the curtain of flakes and dying light.

By that time, he reached the second of the valley's knolls. At its base grew a tight semicircle of Canadian spruce with branches full of long, drooping fingers that could provide some shelter from the storm. He made directly for the trees.

The nearby knoll, unlike the first, was not heavily treed. Only three spruce grew on its summit, but there were a few dead trees at its base. He began to chop wood, piling it just outside the semicircle of spruce. There were two pines nearby whose lower trunks were spiked with dead branches, and he broke these off.

He gathered as much wood as he could, knowing it had to last the night, maybe longer. Better to be safe while he had time. If only his strength would hold out.

Finally, when the wood was piled higher than his waist and as long as his body, he circled the Canadian spruce and entered a hollow behind. It was three times as long as his body. He crawled close to the trunks and bent away the branches that protruded into his shelter. But, because the branches were green, he was unable to break them, so he used his hatchet to clear a space where he could reach his woodpile

His hands were stiff with cold, yet functioning, but the chill within him was deep and hard, and a tiredness had settled in his body, heavy, like a sea of mud.

He pulled the birch bark from his pocket, and the demolished compass spilled onto the floor of brown spruce needles. He tore off a swatch of bark, which he shredded into filaments. Over this, he piled kindling and then larger pieces of wood. The wood outside the trees was already covered with snow, and a couple of inches lay on the ground.

He started his fire with one match, and then he settled and watched the snow through the branches. Even the three trees behind him on the mound were nearly obliterated, the air crowded with flakes that were driven by no wind, but falling fast and thick of their own volition.

How fast it was piling up. A couple of inches already, and it had just begun. He'd have to be sure not to jar the trees and cause an avalanche. He didn't have many matches, and even one match was too high a price to pay for carelessness.

The fire burned hot, but barely touched his coldness, and the smoke, impeded by the trees, burned his eyes, making them water. He felt sick from breathing the smoke, and he shuddered, the nausea swelling within him.

God, he'd be in fine shape, wouldn't he, if he couldn't keep any food down. He'd have to make the acorns last. He'd forgotten to look for food.

The world was silent, except for the crackle of the fire. The dizziness in his head was pulling him into a nether world, smoky and dreamy, with the fire burning heatless somewhere beyond its fringe. The cold shuddered through him again as he listened to the pop and crackle of the fire. But suddenly his senses bristled, and he sat up, stiff and alert. But there was only the distant pulse of his heart, and the popping fire, and the silent pandemonium of snow.

He had sensed it, though; there was no denying it. Something watching him.

He peered through the drooping branches but saw nothing but falling flakes.

Maybe it was the souls of the dead his old man talked about. Too bad if it was. He had never learned to listen with his heart like his old man told him, like his old man could. Maybe now he could do it, too. Maybe he could now that he had admitted the truth about himself.

He chuckled without joy.

And if not? He stopped thinking a moment. Then, soon, he would be one of those souls. Maybe then he would understand.

Why couldn't he warm up? If he fed the fire, maybe it would drive that feeling out. If he felt better, maybe it would go away.

The fire seemed so distant now. The wood he pulled in from outside the trees was real enough. He could feel that with his hands. But when he placed the wood onto the fire, it was like he reached into another dimension that would let all things in, yet would let nothing out, except firelight.

A feeling, like coldness, but not coldness, flickered along the edges of his shivering, and his lightheadedness swirled in slowly widening arcs.

What was the matter with him? He was a woodsman, wasn't

he? What was there to be afraid of?

He was afraid, though, wasn't he?

He wasn't going to die. He wouldn't let himself die. It was as easy as that. If you didn't give in, it couldn't take your life from you. It couldn't.

Christ, it all seemed a muddle. And his head. Please, god, make the swirling stop. He had to think. He couldn't think with it going around and around. And the cold. Damn he was cold. More wood. He ought to add more wood.

He shivered and dragged in more wood and fed the fire and then huddled close to it. The shivering was reaching deeper into him, with cold, probing fingers.

It was out there again. God, look how his hands were shaking.

He wiped one hand over his mouth.

It was like when he was a kid. Afraid of the darkness. He remembered how it scared him to go into his room at night, how, when he was old enough, he would rush to the lantern with the match already drawn, fearing he would feel something reach out of the darkness before he could strike the match. And then, when the lantern was lit, he sensed that something was behind him, and, when he turned, he would see some hideous thing huddled in the corner of his room.

"Stay away!"

His voice died instantly, smothered in sagging branches and the riotous fall of snow. The sensation passed, and he felt alone again, so very alone and lost.

He was aware of his tiredness, how his eyes were growing heavy-lidded. He shook his head, trying to drive the feeling away.

He couldn't let himself sleep. What if it came while he was asleep? If he stayed awake, maybe it couldn't touch him.

He struggled to stay awake. It was dark, and the snow was still falling, and there was a carpet of snow in his shelter, though the trees were protecting him as he hoped. The sky and the wilderness were softly aglow with the weak fluorescence of snow, and after awhile his nervousness eased, eased a little more, then sank into the muck of his exhaustion...

"David." It was not one voice, but thousands. And not in unison. The voices sounded full of wind.

It was black behind his eyelids.

"David," the voices surged and sighed.

He felt something, someone, touch his eyelids—a gentle pressure.

He could see a room then, murky, but not in total darkness, faint light entering from the left. The room had gray stone walls and an earthen floor.

A cellar.

He could see a slender figure standing in the darkness, a woman, her back toward him. She wore a long, white, dressing gown, and her hair was pinned in a bun, exposing her neck. She turned.

Carrie! And she was crying.

He watched as she pulled a wooden chair closer to her, and mounted it, and raised her arms over her head. She was reaching toward what?

A beam. And now he could see the rope, too. He watched as she wrapped the rope twice around the beam, and knotted it, and then pulled to confirm that it was secure. She turned, and he could see her face again. She was sobbing, and her body shook with the depth of her grief, but there was no sound.

There was a loop at the end of the rope. She looked at it a long time, still sobbing. Then she glanced upward and sighed and mouthed something. He could not hear what she said, but he could see her lips. It looked like: "I'm sorry, ____," with the third word indecipherable but, he thought, beginning with the letter dee. Then, abruptly, she slipped the loop over her head and, without hesitating, raised her arms and grasped the rope above her and lifted her body free of the chair. She kicked the chair away. He could not hear any sound as it tumbled into the dirt. Then she let go of the rope.

He watched her hang a moment, utterly still. But then something appeared to go terribly wrong. Her eyes shot open, bulging, and he could see the terror. She convulsed once, hard, and desperately reached above for the rope. Grasping it, she pulled her body up. For a few moments, she clung, her feet kicking as she struggled to keep the pressure off her neck, to wriggle free of the noose. Gradually, however, she lost strength, and he watched her fingers slide down the rope until, finally, they let go. Again she kicked and tried to grasp the rope, to get her fingers under the noose. He watched her thrash and kick. Then her fingers loosened and her arms slowly dropped to her sides. Her body went limp then, and she swung in the silence of the semidarkness until there was no movement at all.

"Carrie." He started from his sleep, panting. His eyes darted, then fixed on his fire. The fire danced, the flames small and scattered. He exhaled and shook his head and then breathed heavily again.

Where had that come from? Sweet jesus.

He covered his mouth with his hand, then dabbed at his eyes with his other hand.

Thank god he only dreamed it. But it seemed so real.

He tilted his head up, squinting, then looked into the branches.

He didn't want that for her. She could be gone from him forever if that's what she wanted, but he could not bear to think of her... not like that.

He needed to add wood to the fire.

He paused.

But what if it was true? What would make her do that?

No, she couldn't do that. She wouldn't. Yet this seemed so much more than a dream. And the voices, and his eyelids? He didn't imagine that, and it gave him the willies.

"Oh, Carrie. I pray that's not what happened to you. With all my heart."

He wiped his eyes.

So he wouldn't think about her that way then. He would think about her as he preferred, in his arms. And he would stroke her hair and cheek, and kiss her forehead.

Enough.

He jerked into a sitting position. His fire had burned low.

He pulled in wood through the branches and knocked the snow from each piece. There had to be at least a half-foot of snow, and the bitterness of his luck clenched his heart.

The fire revived and breathed lowly, and he could feel the flames touching the chill in him and make him yearn for sleep.

There was no sense getting angry about the snow. He would deal with that in the morning. Now he wanted to sleep and dream about his Carrie. Carrie folded in his arms, where nothing could ever hurt her. He never again wanted to think about her as in his dream, and he vowed he never would. Still, there was something that left him trembling and fearful that what he had seen was true.

August 1919

She was holding the stemmed glass to her lips. The late-summer sun shone through the window and burned in her brown hair. She looked at him from above the rim of the glass with the same vacant, dull eyes he had hoped would be different tonight. Her eyes were clear and her nose was pale and delicate through the water in the glass.

"You've been quiet this evening," she said, her voice muted and nearly buzzing through the glass.

"I guess so. Seems we both have."

She set her glass on the white tablecloth. "You've hardly touched your dinner, either. Isn't it all right?"

"Oh, sure. Just not very hungry I guess." He looked out the window. The street was quiet, empty, except for a stooped old woman walking with a cane. "This isn't how I thought it would be," he said, looking at her.

She sighed. "I know. Goodbyes seldom are."

"I thought we would talk. When haven't we been able to?"

She shrugged. "Maybe it's because it's all been said."

He let his head go back; then he exhaled. "No, there are things left to say. It's this place. It was a bad choice."

"David, please don't start. Not tonight of all nights."

"Well, I am doing better than last time. There's a memory."

"Don't think about it then."

"But I embarrassed you so."

"You didn't at all."

"I was embarrassed. You had to be."

"I wish you'd stop that. Stop attributing feelings to me. When I'm embarrassed, I'll let you know."

"That's right. That's good. Let's fight."

"You're the one who keeps bringing up this foolishness."

" Good lord, Carrie, I didn't even know what fork to use. And in front of your friends. We always used just one."

"Stop it, will you please!"

Then he saw that her eyes were filling. He watched her suck in a pained breath and then swallow.

"I'm sorry." He touched her hand gently.

She nodded. "It's that I just can't take it," she said, choking the words out.

"Carrie, I'm sorry." He looked at the table. "I didn't mean to upset you. I just can't bear the thought of losing you."

"You're not losing me," she said. "I told you that on Pine Cobble. How many times do I have to say it?"

"I know. I know. But it's more. It's the feeling... Mostly, it's the fear... that this is the last time I'll ever see you."

"That's nonsense!" She peered out the window and tapped her finger against the table. Then she looked at him, her eyes brimming. "David, I do understand what you're feeling. But I have to put it—you—aside for awhile. I just can't bear all that I am right now and your pain, too. I've told you, it's got to wait. Just till I sort out my life and find direction again."

"But six months? Why must it be so long?"

"Because I need the time... I know it will take that much time."

"How can you?"

"Because I do!" Then she was crying.

"Carrie, what is it?" he asked, taking one of her hands. "Every time we talk about this, either you get angry or you come apart."

She shook her head and waved her hand.

"I don't suppose it makes much difference. Even if you come back, we'll never be more to each other than we are."

"We don't know what the future holds," she squeaked.

"Don't we?"

"She exhaled a deep breath. "David, you're different. Different doesn't mean inferior."

"Different? That's an understatement."

"Enough. For god's sake, can't you see you're killing me!"

Why in hell was he doing this?

Then he was quiet for a long time, listening to her cry.

"I guess I love you so much it's making me crazy. That's why I'm saying these things. It's just that if I lose you altogether... I don't know what I'd do. I'm so afraid of that."

"But it's not for good. I've told you. David, if I don't have this time, I'm not going to make it. I'm sorry it means separating from you, but your pain is another burden right now, and I'm not strong enough to bear it. And if you force me to, it will crush me. Is that what you want?"

He looked into her brimming eyes. "No. You know I don't." They were both quiet a moment. "I'll need to hear from you."

She shook her head.

"Carrie!"

"I can't, David. To me there is no difference. Your pain on paper would be as real, and I have to get away from it."

"But don't ask that of me, too."

"I must."

"Carrie, please."

She closed her eyes and held her hands over her mouth and nose. "All right," she said. "I will write to you. When I can. But no letters in return. I can't let you know where I am."

He turned and looked out the window. The street was lined with elms, and the dying sun was behind them now, glowing orange through the black leaves and branches. Then he looked down at his plate. A moment later she touched his hand.

"David? My god, you're trembling."

He took his hand away and looked into her eyes. Hers were they only eyes he had ever trusted, except his mother's, the only eyes he had ever looked into without feeling the discomfort that pulled his eyes away.

Just then the waiter was by the table. He saw the blue jacket out of the corner of his eye. The waiter stood still, looking out the window, until it was obvious that he had been noticed. Carrie dried her eyes.

"Will there be anything else, sir?" the waiter asked. "A digestif for you and the lady perhaps."

He shot a look to Carrie, who shook her head almost imperceptibly.

"No," he replied.

"Very well, sir." The waiter turned.

"Ah, thanks," he said to the waiter's back.

The waiter stopped. "Thank you, sir." He did not look back.

He watched the waiter depart, then exhaled.

"David? You were trembling. What is it?"

He hesitated, then he shook his head.

"Please."

He swallowed. "It's... It's that I feel so lost sometimes, Carrie. So different from everyone else. Like I'm not a whole person. I... I..." He turned away. "I don't know whether I can say this."

"Try." She touched his hand.

"Carrie. I want someone to love me, and I want someone to love in return. I'm so afraid that's never going to happen. No one ever has ever loved me, except maybe my mother, in the way mothers do. And I hardly remember her."

She squeezed his hand and was quiet a long time. Then she said: "I know. But before that can happen, you'll have to learn to stop hating yourself. Do you realize that? And I won't ever abandon you, David. I promise. I would have to abandon myself first."

The words, her touch, did not wholly register. All he could see was the waiter, the thin, ramrod-straight waiter, looking down his nose with those condescending eyes.

DAY THREE

11

He woke shivering and eyed his fire without lifting his head. The fire was a smoking mound.

He propped himself on one elbow and rubbed the sleep from his eyes, but when he looked, he nearly fell forward. He shook his head hard and looked again, but the dizziness persisted.

Before he laid back, he gathered several small branches and stirred the gray ashes, uncovering a bed of embers. Then he turned onto his stomach and, digging his fingers through the covering of spruce needles, pulled himself a few inches closer to his woodpile. He cried out suddenly and jerked back.

The splint. It had snagged on a root.

The pain settled slowly, and his breath shook as he exhaled. For a moment, the pain had driven the dizziness from his head, but now it started to circle as before.

He needed to be careful. He couldn't give all his strength to the pain. He'd need it when it was time to press on.

Making certain not to snag the splint, he reached through the branches to the piled wood. His hand closed on the first squat log. It was cold, blanketed with snow, but when he pulled, it did not move. He yanked on the log once, twice, and then, abruptly, it came free, shooting through the branches and striking him on the forehead. It covered his face with snow, and the snow burned on his skin. He wiped the snow away on his sleeve.

For an instant, because of the blow, he felt lost in the middle of his actions, not recollecting what it was he was doing. Then he saw the log in his hand.

He ought to put that on the fire. "Ha-ha."

Before moving, he licked the snow from his mustache. It was deliciously cold, and he savored its wetness.

He broke some small branches and put them into the fire and, when they were burning, picked up the log. He held the log with his arms cocked, his elbows on the ground, and tried to steady it. He watched the log meander from one side of the fire to the other. He tried to shake off the dizziness and made another pass, dropping the log over the flames. It hit the embers with an eruption of sparks and rolled to the fire's edge.

With his hand shaking, he dragged the log back into the fire.

One wasn't enough, he told himself, shivering. He needed to throw on lots of wood. When he got warm again, he'd be all right. But he would need a big fire.

Walking his forearms to one side, he turned back toward the woodpile and tugged out another piece of wood. This time he propped himself on one elbow and tried to place the wood on the fire. His hand shook, and his dizziness almost pulled him off balance. He let go of the wood. It hit and settled, sparks filling the shelter like glowing snowflakes.

Right in the middle. Good. Good.

He gathered three more pieces, and he managed to get each into the fire, but now he was tired. He rested, listening to the wood hiss as the moisture within boiled. The flames leapt higher, almost touching the spruce branches, but the heat did not reach to the depth of his coldness. He could feel the heat on his skin but, inside, he felt as cold as a cave, with his shivering starting deep in the darkness.

He wished his old man were here. He'd get him warm. There wasn't anything he couldn't do out here.

It was better thinking about him now. It was good to try to remember some good things. But there were so few.

That was both their faults, he supposed.

He remembered, as a kid, he'd ride on his old man's shoulders, his legs around his neck. That was one good memory. He remembered how his old man's neck was all scruffy. And he could remember not wanting to grow up when he was up there because it scared him to be that high, and he wondered if it scared his old man to have his head that far from the ground. But his old man always held him by the ankles so he wouldn't fall, and then it didn't scare him as much.

Usually it was Sunday mornings when they would walk like that. After church. He'd watch his old man unhitch the horses. And his mother, she'd go inside to fix Sunday dinner.

It was the only day he could recall him resting. Not the whole day. But he didn't do any work until after dinner at noon.

He would let the horses loose in the fenced pasture by the barn. Then they'd walk. His old man would come up behind, and hoist him skyward and drop him over his head. That's what scared him most, watching the ground rush away, upside down, until he dropped right side up onto those boney shoulders, and his old man grabbed him around the ankles.

And he could remember the easy movements of the body beneath him. Sometimes he'd pretend he was riding an elephant. He imagined it must feel like that, slow and lumbering.

They'd climb the hill behind the house and cross the meadow. And he'd looked behind to see where his old man's feet had flattened the grass.

Then they'd start to climb, the same hill every Sunday. A high hill, wooded, so he couldn't see anything until they reached the top. Sometimes his old man would duck so the branches wouldn't hit him in the face. "Watch out for that one," he'd call up, and he'd duck down near his head and could smell the pomade that he always put on before Sunday Mass. The only day he wore it.

At the top of the hill was a clearing, and they could see all the land around them, the roofs of the house and barn, and all the rolling mountains in the distance, all the trees, thousands of trees.

For a while they'd just look. He could remember the quiet. Maybe only a bird twittering. Then his old man would say something. He remembered because he said the same thing every time, even years later, repeating it like the refrain from a song.

"This is what I respect."

That was the word: respect.

"Your mama," he once said years after his mother was dead. "She had her church and her God. This here is my church. If you can't feel God here, can't believe you'll feel Him anywhere."

After his mother died, his old man didn't go to church anymore. And after that, long, long after, when Emma questioned him about it, about not seeing that his son had religion, his old man told her that he didn't want them to have anything to do with a God that would take his Ellie away. He couldn't believe in that kind of a

God and sure as hell wouldn't worship Him.

As a boy, though, sometimes he'd go off to the church without letting his old man know, but if he was looking for something there, he never found it.

He shivered and held one hand to the fire. Slowly, the heat ate its way inward.

Respect. His old man didn't give that easily. Far as he knew, he only respected two things in his life. The woods... and men who could get on in the woods like he could.

He could remember him squeezing his ankles when he said the word. Funny to remember a thing like that after all these years. Why was it he never remembered things like that before? Now, it seemed like a good thing to share, the two of them in the solitude.

He could even remember his old man's voice, how it said the words from below. It was an easy sound, deep, almost like it was the earth saying the words.

Then his old man would set him down, and they'd sit against a rock, and he would load up his corncob and smoke, usually not speaking again, just taking in the trees and the beautiful roll of mountains. Sometimes he'd pat him on the knee, but not saying anything. Was he having some kind of secret thought? He wished he knew now. But his old man wasn't the talking sort.

But there was one time that he remembered especially. That evening on the front porch the summer that he died. His old man was sitting in one of the straight-backed wooden chairs, balanced on its rear legs. His feet were on the rail, and he was smoking his corncob, its stem clamped between his teeth so he didn't need his hands to hold it. His arms were folded on his chest, and he was just looking off into the darkness.

He was sitting next to him, his feet on the rail, too. His chair was closer. His legs weren't as long, but almost.

The only light came from the windows behind, so his old man's face was in shadow, the pipe bowl glowing feebly when he sucked.

Just beyond the porch he could hear the heavy drone of a June bug, and farther beyond, below the chirping crickets, the baritone croaking of the bullfrogs from the pond.

"Like music," his old man said.

He didn't answer. He hadn't expected him to speak. He almost always just sat there, puffing and staring.

"Yeah. I suppose it is, kind of."

Then it was the same again. There was only the seething of the pipe stem when he sucked.

"Sure it is," he said moments later. "More like music than that stuff you young people listen to these days. Whaddayah call it?"

"I dunno," he'd answered. "You mean ragtime?"

"Yeah, that's it. Just noise. This is just noise, too. But kind of peaceful. Makes you feel easy, like music should.

"Your mama. She always said that. She loved to set out here and jus' listen. Set in that rocker over there. I remember how it use to squeak. Fit right in with the rest of them sounds. Always said she couldn't think of no finer way to end a day than just a setting here and a listening with me by..."

He never finished it. He removed the pipe from his mouth and, leaning forward, spat over the rail. Then he reinserted the pipe and leaned back. But there wasn't any more.

He wasn't sure. Had he heard a catch in his voice? And when he looked, a sidelong glance, were his eyes glistening, or had he just imagined it?

He hadn't dared look again and, in awhile, he stopped hearing the silence and started hearing the sounds again—the buzzings and chirpings, and from behind the house, from the woods across the meadow, the hooting of the horned owl that frequented there.

To this day he never knew whether there had been tears in his old man's eyes. He didn't really remember either what his old man had said on those mornings on the hillside. But it would be about the woods, the voice coming out slow and easy and deep. He'd felt easy too, but also a little like a pea sitting next to a boulder.

Now he just felt cold. And dizzy. It was because he had not had enough to drink. He knew the effects of dehydration well enough.

The fire was a blotch of wavering orange, and then his reverie departed and his eyes focused. His stomach wavered like the fire.

He repositioned himself. The pain in his leg was a constant fire and the movement only aggravated it, but he needed to get warm. Now he sat with his legs out straight, the fire between, and he held out his hands.

He saw the compass lying on the brown needles. He had forgotten to put it away, and now he retrieved it, pressing the mangled metal in his hands before he slipped the compass into his vest pocket. It had taken twenty-five years, or almost, but finally he felt a connection to it.

Now he remembered the snow and peered out through the branches. His head circled, but he could see that it was still snowing, the flakes like down in the air. It was not snowing hard, and it was dawn. Hadn't he told himself to get moving at dawn? Ah, Christ, who knew what he had told himself?

He clutched himself and rocked back and forth.

He remembered finding a deer once, dead, frozen, its head in a stream but still wearing that same peaceful, big-eyed deer look that deer wear. It looked like it was just resting.

He wouldn't freeze. He had a fire, so he wouldn't freeze.

He clutched himself and stared at the fire.

How many fires could he remember in his life?

Too many. The fires of his private Hell. There was the one on the night he was twelve and his old man gave him the compass, and the one the next night that he made too large because he was afraid. And the fire the night his old man took him to his grandfather's spot in the woods. And the one on the night his mother died. And ones even before that because he remembered now that she would read to him before the fire, or sometimes sing or play games, or the pattacake rhyme when she would make his hands clap in time.

So many memories. Maybe that's what life boiled down to, memories reaching to the far end of your life only so you could look back, like looking down a corridor. And regret them? Good god, did he regret them, because of the hating? Because he knew now that he'd been wrong?

And what about this fire? What would this fire mean? And would he have any reason to remember it?

"Son of a bitching fire. Warm me, for christ sake. Warm me! Act like a sensible, goddamn fire!"

He pulled back from the fire and swung his right leg close to his left, the pain leaping. He rolled over and reclined by the fire.

There were no more nights by the fire after his mother died. Because his old man sat there, and he didn't want to be near him.

He could have had a brother, or a sister, if his mother had lived. Sometimes he'd pretend he had brother.

Why?

He didn't know. But it was a brother he pretended. Maybe because a brother would want to do the same things he wanted to do. It would have been good. Then his old man would have two. It

183

was so hard being the only one. You could try to be better than your brother. And being older, he could. But you couldn't be better than your father, or even as good, no matter how hard you tried.

His brother's name was Jim. He could imagine his old man talking to Jim: "No, Jim, that's not right. Why can't you do it like David? Watch David." And then he'd show Jim, and he'd do it right, whatever it was. Building a fire, using a compass, reading a map.

Poor Jim just wouldn't be able to do it, and he'd show him because he was older and smarter and because his old man had already taught him. And his old man would be better, more patient, because he could see how much better he was than Jim.

Why hadn't Jim lived? Why both Jim and his mother?

He gripped himself hard and stared into the fire, and the tongues of flame blurred and ran together.

No one to talk to. That was the hardest thing. The god awful loneliness.

With Jim, he would have had someone. His old man didn't talk. The woods were the only thing he really communicated with. After his mother died, the woods seemed like the only thing his old man cared about. But was that true, or had the night she died put the two of them beyond reach forever? Did it matter to him whether his old man loved him? How many ways could people express love, or disguise it? So much, though, as to make it unrecognizable?

Did it matter?

He looked at the snow in the branches of the spruce.

Yeah. It mattered plenty.

Thirsty. Damn he was thirsty.

If Jim was here, he could send him for water. If he didn't do it, he'd tell his old man. Then Jim would catch it for a change. He was tired of catching it.

God, what in hell was he talking about?

He felt like he was drunk. He was drunk only once in his life, but he remembered how it felt, how the jail cell swung around and around whenever he closed his eyes. That goddamn Dick. He's the one who got him drunk. His one big trip to Montreal. Dick spoke French. Had French Canadian ancestors or something. The two of them went on a binge and then wound up in a restaurant. The waitress they had was so pretty. He remembered that much, and that she only spoke French. That goddamn Dick. The waitress said something to him in French.

"What did she say?" he asked Dick.

"She asked who my friend was. Says you're kind of cute."

"Oh, yeah. Well I think she's downright, goddamn, extraordinary beautiful. You tell her that for me. G'won. Do it nice, though."

Dick said something to the waitress.

"Oui," the waitress answered.

Dick said something else, and then the waitress wedged her tray under her arm and held her hands about one foot apart

"What's goin' on?" he asked Dick.

"I asked her if she'd like to go to bed with you. She said yes. Then I asked her if she could guess how big your donger was. I'd say she's overestimating a bit, wouldn't you?"

But Dick didn't wait for an answer. He said something else to the waitress, and she answered: "Oui."

Dick turned back to him and said: "I just asked her if she'd like to see Davy Junior right here in this restaurant. She said yes."

Hell, he was so drunk, it sounded half reasonable. So he stood up and unzipped his trousers when all of a sudden the waitress starts screaming bloody murder. One minute later he and Dick are out on the sidewalk. Then that son of a bitch gets to laughing.

"Ha-ha-ha-ha-ha," he says, lying next to him. "Know what... Know what we was really saying?"

"No, goddamn it."

"I asked her if... ha-ha... if they served garlic bread. And she says yes. So then I asked how big a loaf was. Ha-ha-ha-ha-ha. That's when she put her hands in the air like that. So then I asked if she thought the two of us could finish a loaf that big. Sure we could. And that's when you stood up and started to show her Davy Junior." Dick roared. "Probably would have let you if only she realized it's better lookin' than your face. What a goddamn ugly bastard you are. I ever tell you that?"

"Why you..." And then he chased Dick down the street until the two of them tumbled headlong into a row of trash cans. They spent that night in jail.

Goddamn, that crazy son of a bitch. He hoped he lived long enough to see him again.

He shivered, and his eyes focused on the fire.

Eating something hot. Maybe that would help.

He didn't feel like eating, though.

He had acorns. Crummy acorns. Just as soon eat these spruce needles. He could get the acorns hot but sure didn't feel like fixing them. He wished he had someone to do it for him.

Hey, Jim, fix these acorns.

Jim. He'd do anything. Chain of command. That's how families worked. Younger ones minding older ones. Mothers minding fathers because fathers were bosses.

Not aunts, though. Aunts did what the hell they wanted. Emma did, anyway.

His old man was funny with her. He looked at her funny. Not all the time, but enough. He'd seen it in his eyes when he thought no one was watching. Like it hurt him to have to look at her.

He felt the same way sometimes. He knew his old man was seeing his Ellie. He never said anything, though. He always kept his feelings inside. Except anger. That came out easy. But that was okay for men. Sadness and tears were for women.

Poor old man. Tough to be a man, to have to go on acting like a man no matter what. Women, mothers… they had it easier. It was okay for them to be all the things fathers couldn't be.

Jim, those acorns.

Ha, what was he thinking?

Poor Jim. Sometimes he could actually see him. They were boys. Jim running across the meadow, his curly hair bouncing, his clothes a little baggy because they were hand-me-downs.

They'd wrestle in the grass. Of course, he could always beat Jim. He was bigger. But sometimes he'd pretend to lose. He'd do it so well Jim didn't catch on. He'd do it because he knew it was important to win. Everyone needed to win once in awhile.

Then they'd talk about things. Sitting there in the grass that was higher than their heads. Jim would be the curious sort. Ask a thousand questions. Especially about Mother and what happened. He'd tell Jim it wasn't his fault. Wasn't anyone's fault. Silly to blame himself. After all, he didn't ask to be born. He could just ask Emma if he didn't believe it wasn't his fault.

Why didn't Emma come more often? She didn't come to the funeral, but he found out later that his old man hadn't told her. Wasn't much of a funeral. Just the priest and a few neighbors to help with the coffin. He'd seen from his bedroom window.

He hadn't been allowed to go. How would his old man have explained the bruises?

By the time Emma came that summer, the bruises were gone. The ones outside, anyway. But Emma was too upset about the death and the funeral to notice. That was the first time he ever saw her. He thought it was his mother come back. Can you imagine?

Acorns. He ought to heat them. Get something hot into him.

But just then there was a rustling above, followed by a "caw, caw, caw, caw, caw," and he looked up to see the snow sliding from branch to branch and then drop squarely onto his fire.

March 1920

March 16, 1920
44 Pleasant Street
Plymouth, Wisconsin

Dearest Louise:

It is done. God forgive me. I fear I shall hate myself for eternity. What kind of a mother gives her child away? And yet I have done that to my baby, my Matthew.

Louise, you cannot imagine how it hurts. I believe the pain may kill me. I keep wondering, what if Jim were to look upon the perfect little miracle that he is, to hold him in his arms, just once, and feel him soft against him? Surely it would melt the coldest heart. Surely he would come back to me then. To us. But now it is too late.

Louise, I am shattered and so confused. Aunt Agatha assures me that what I have done is best for Matthew, tries tirelessly to convince me that the situation with Jim is hopeless. She says only a coward or a scoundrel would do what he did. But to believe that, to believe that we mean nothing to him, is to abandon all hope. Consciously, I struggle toward accepting that he is gone forever, but I do not believe my heart will ever accept it. And how can I possibly hope to accept what I have done to my Matthew?

It all seems too much: Papa's death, Jim's leaving, and now Matthew. No person should have to bear all this at the same time. I just want to come home. But I would not wish you or Paul and the children to see me like this.

Never see him again! Have you ever heard such a hopeless word as never!

Please tell me there is hope. Tell me honestly you would have done what I have done.

There is so much on my mind. David has been on my mind, too. I have not written. Just one letter from the train. I trust you have done what I asked and told him that I think of him often and still care for him deeply. Please make him understand that I will be in touch just as soon as I am well. He has been such a dear friend and cares for me so. Tell him whatever you need to comfort him. Perhaps when this is over, and with the passing of time, I can be for him what he wants me to be. But please, not a word about Matthew. I don't want anyone to know about Matthew until I am sure I can live with myself. I am not sure I can.

Louise, please write just as soon as you receive this. I am desperate to hear from you. I need someone to convince me that I am not the monster I feel myself to be.

Carrie.

March 23, 1920
147 Church Street
Bennington, Vermont

Dearest Carrie,

Have received yours of March 16 with much distress. Good Lord, get a grip on yourself. I know you hurt, but you must stop torturing yourself. You have done the right thing, the best thing. I would have done the same, believe me. Do not think for one moment that I am saying this because you asked me to. I am saying this for one reason: it is the truth.

If I were there right now, I would give you a good slap and tell you to get on with your life. Don't over-intellectualize. You have done what is right and best—period. Move on!

Think. What kind of a life could you offer Matthew? Would you want him to live with the shame surrounding his birth? How would you support yourself? You are hardly more than a child yourself. You have not even finished your education, which you must do, as Papa wanted.

Do not think me harsh for saying these things, but someone has to give it to you straight. If you are honest, you will have to agree: a child needs a family (both a mother and a father), where it can be loved and not grow up hurt and confused about its birth and the absence of a father.

Carrie, it has taken great strength to do what you have done. Reach inside one more time. In time, you'll see, your pain will ease, and you will be happy knowing that Matthew has been placed in a loving home. What more selfless act could a mother commit on her child's behalf?

Paul and I and the children miss you. So get yourself well. If Aunt Agatha tells me otherwise, rest assured, I will be on the first train to Plymouth to slap some sense into you.

Your sister,

Louise

P.S.

There is no need to concern yourself about David. He has departed Bennington. He wrote Emma a touching note. She showed it to me. Not much in it, just some personal things between them. Emma says not to worry. She doesn't know why he left, but she's sure he is fine. Good riddance, I say. I don't know what you saw in him, but I am glad you did not encourage him. Of course, he pestered me about your whereabouts, but I would not tell. I did nothing to encourage him. In fact, just the opposite. I told him you did not want to hear from him... ever! That seemed to take him down a peg or two. Anyway, you are well rid of him. You would do well to put him out of your mind. Lord knows you have demons enough to torment you.

12

He lay on his back, utterly still, staring dumbly at the remains of his fire—a hill of smoking snow, with scorched wood protruding. The snow's impact had blown a dusting of ash onto his shirtsleeve and vest, and he brushed it away, his head swimming as he watched the movements of his hand.

It didn't matter, he told himself. He was supposed to get going at dawn, and it was after dawn. He had to try.

He propped himself on one elbow and peered through the branches. There was daylight, and snow. The world was white.

He strained to sit up. It felt as if someone were restraining him by the shoulders, but up his body came, shaking with the exertion. Nearby, nearly hidden in the snow that had come in under the branches, was his crutch. He leaned to reach it, and his movements felt distant, dreamy, and it seemed to take an hour before his hand closed on the crutch. Then he rolled onto his stomach and watched the tree trunks circle slowly. He turned his face downward, his forehead on his arm as he tried to calm the queasiness in his stomach. Everything seemed distant now, the press of his forehead, the quiet of his breathing. Even the scent of the spruce needles.

It reminded him of Christmas. Sneaking to the stairs. Coming down just far enough to watch. Mother in the chair. Stringing popcorn from a bowl in her lap. Watching her hand poke the needle through the kernels. Giving the string to his old man. He put it on the tree, grumbling. Didn't make sense to put food on a tree. And then his mother laughing. "If you don't want it to go to waste, Jacob, you can eat it... just as soon as Christmas is over."

And his old man not doing anything at first, just looking, until she smiled. And then smiling, he went to her and gave her a hug.

He remembered another Christmas. When Emma came. They hadn't had a tree since his mother died.

Remembered his old man opening the door, Emma barging past. "Come on, Eric. Bring it in here." And Eric brought in the balsam. He knew it was a balsam because his old man was teaching him.

What the hell did she think she was doing? This was his home, not hers. Their usual go 'round. But Emma always did pretty much what she wanted. And poor Uncle Eric. Setting the tree up. Then down because his old man wouldn't have it. Up, down.

Finally it was Emma who won. Then she sat in the chair and strung popcorn. His old man sat across from her, silent. Later, he noticed him looking at Emma. He could see that look even now, like he was looking at a ghost. He wondered what he was thinking. But it didn't last long because just then Emma stood and badgered him until he got up and helped with the decorating. They let him put the star at the tree top, his old man holding him up so he could reach. He could still feel the boney fingers pushing into his ribs.

After Christmas, taking the tree down, he said to his old man that he liked having a Christmas tree again.

"Emma ought to mind her own damn business," he answered. But his tone sounded opposite his meaning.

He shivered violently.

Hell, he was wasting time.

Grasping the crutch, he crawled under the branches, up to the plateau of snow ringing the spruces. It was more than a foot high.

With the crutch, he cleared the snow in front and looked out. The wilderness was white and silent, his breathing the only sound.

A few yards ahead was a fallen tree; a spruce he thought, covered with snow. Near it, there was another tree, still standing. It was about the size of a man, with two branches jutting like arms from either side.

The sky was clearing. The clouds were gray and black, fringed with glowing white from the invisible sun. Blue showed through in patches as the wind high up slowly shredded the clouds.

As he crawled into the snow, his back brushed against a branch, and snow fell onto his neck, scalding him with coldness. He plowed forward, desperate to get the snow off. As he pushed clear of the trees, a spasm of shivering shook him. He wallowed in the deep snow, battering a depression in the otherwise perfect blanket.

He had to get out of the snow. If he could only get to the fallen tree, he could steady himself and shake the snow off and get his bearing.

He tried to pull himself to his feet with the crutch. The point sank, penetrating to the ground, but when he pulled, he slipped and fell into the snow.

The sky swam. He closed his eyes and tried once more, this time wedging his forearm between the tines. With quick, short jumps, his right foot struggled to get under him. A moment later he was standing, unsteadily.

He could not see his foot. The snow was up to his knee.

He moved the crutch forward, through the snow which, though deep, was also light. It did not exert much drag on the crutch.

Because of the dizziness, he moved carefully. His left hand and arm felt weak, and he tightened his grip. In a few minutes, he reached the tree. He grasped a branch and steadied himself.

The trees against the mountains and sky were laden with white—the wilderness, the valley, silent—the snow having muffled the earth. The only sound was his hushed panting.

Down the valley, the trees were thin, scattered, the branches of the evergreens only blotches of green now under a lading of white, and on the mountains, the brown tree trunks stood like ten thousand match sticks. The stand of three spruces on the knoll nearby was blue-green beneath a covering of snow.

He could see the mountain at the far end of the valley. Somehow, the snow made it look more distant than yesterday, maybe because the brown tree trunks were distinct now, and they were so tiny, so numberless.

Now what? he asked. Should he go on, or go back and wait?

Wait for what? Dick wasn't coming. And what chance would he have of finding him? He had to go on like he promised. If the going was too tough, he could come back.

He put his right hand under his arm and leaned his weight on the crutch. As he hopped forward, his toe caught, and he fell, face first, through cracking tree branches, into the snow.

He struggled to turn over. Digging his right foot in, he pushed onto his side. Beneath him, his left hand was going raw, and his wrist hurt. His head circled.

Let go of the crutch, you idiot.

He concentrated, visualized opening his hand and sliding his arm out. And then, suddenly, his arm was free.

He blew on his fingers, amazed how red they were after such a short exposure. His breath shivered out, but its warmth had no effect his fingers could feel. The snow was cold against his body.

He drew a deep breath and, concentrating on gathering his strength, pushed with his elbow. It sank away from him and then stopped when the snow packed beneath it, and a moment later he was on his back, looking at the sky.

Once more he pushed with his elbow. His left hand flailed as he tried to rise. Then something grabbed his wrist.

With his mind circling, he fought to follow his arm to his hand. He shrugged his cheeks, then looked.

A branch. He was caught in a branch. "Ha-ha-ha."

He stopped pulling and slid his hand up and out. Shivering, he looked at the sky but had to close his eyes against the dark commotion. The dizziness was moving into him again, stirring in his stomach. He shivered and was sure he could feel his body enlarging its hollow in the snow.

Please oh please, God, let him get up.

He pushed once more with his elbows. Finally, exhausted, his arms gave up. He sank back.

He'd have to wait. He'd have to rest, then try again.

It was sometime later, between spasms of shivering, that he heard them—the crows. Their voices, distant at first, drew closer, ringing in the frigid and perfect silence. He felt the first cold tingles of fear rush through him on little spider feet. And then he was thrashing in the snow. By degrees, he pushed himself up. When he let his head go back, it hit against a branch and stopped. His body felt wilted, like a plant left too long without water.

The crows were close now, their obscene caws defiling the virgin silence.

He tried to locate them. Then they cawed again, and he saw them at the top of the spruces on the knoll, one on each of the left and rightmost trees. He watched the ugly black forms flapping, lunging and cawing at each other, sending dollops of snow cascading down the branches. Then he had to close his eyes. After that, he just listened. Their voices came through his dizziness with the harshness of train wheels on steel tracks. He blocked his ears.

He wished he could kill them. He wished to god he could.

But soon there was not strength enough to hold his hands over his ears. They dropped, and then he waited, with his head against the branch, and prayed for his strength to come back. And as he waited, his shivering grew more vicious until he was not sure which tormented him more, his shivering, or the fire in his leg, or the unrelenting cawing. And then, in his mind, he saw the specter of the crows, their eyes black as night, the black, obscene crows, waiting, just waiting for it to be over.

* * *

The shivering had gone on and on. He had shivered for hours, he was sure, wave after wave making him quake against a cold that was equally as fierce and indefatigable.

But then it stopped—of a sudden—and now he felt warm. And he thanked God the shivering had ended.

He let his body go limp, and for a long time he rested with his head against the branch. Although he lay still, the valley would not stop moving. It wheeled, vast and saucer-like, outside his head.

He tried to rise, but his head wobbled, and he slipped back, laughing at his drunken feeling. Then, lunging and throwing his left hand forward, he tried once more, but his hand closed upon nothing, and again he fell back.

For a moment, he was quiet against the branch. He felt his mind float out of him. It laughed at him from somewhere far off, harsh, derisive, painful in his ears.

"Weeeee-oooooooo," he sang. He gathered himself and lunged again, trying to follow the laughter. He held himself free of the branch, straining, but then, as if on a fulcrum, his head teetered and went back in a rush, smacking against the branch. His eyes shot open and the wheeling stopped, just long enough to glimpse the brown and white figure standing against the mountains. Then his mind sank into him, and the valley wheeled, and he shut his eyes.

"I shoulda known," he said. He rolled his head on the branch. "Whaddayah wan'? Go 'way. Leaf me 'lone."

He rolled his head and cracked his eyes.

"All righ', stay. I doan care. I doan. I'm-ma... I'm-ma feelin' a li'l sleepy." He laughed. "An' doan spect me to get up. You spect that an' you got lessa leg to stan' on than I do." He whooped and came a little off the branch and then settled back in a fit of coughing, the pain rising in a leg that, somehow, seemed detached from his body.

When the coughing stopped, he let himself go limp. There was no sound, just the buoyant, billowing rush in his head.

"Wha', not even a laugh, Pa?"

There was only silence.

"Well, you nevah were too long on... on sense-a humor." He smiled, but his eyes remained closed.

"Fee-fie-foe-fum!" he called. "Feefiefoefum, my old man's a grumpy bum! Ha-ha-ha-ha-ha." His head careened right, stopping just as coughing took hold again.

"Weeeee-oooooooo. It feels so good. Like floating. It all feels so good. 'Cept my mouth. My mouth feels like hell."

He licked his lips, unable wet them. Then, as if the sensation came from a long way off, he felt coldness against his fingers.

He lifted his heavy, lolling arm and patted his fingers against his lips. As the snow melted, he drew in the wonderful coldness.

His mouth burned for more.

"Pa. Gimme a drink. Please gimme a drink."

He licked his lips and his tongue adhered.

"Pa? You gotta drink?"

He listened, fighting the rush inside his skull. "Jesus, answer me at leas'! Wha' the fuh you come for? To laugh? To say you tole me so!" He went quiet. With the shouting, his stomach leapt, and he could feel it floating uneasily within him. Moments later, it settled heavily in his bowels.

The wheeling was gaining speed, and he had the strangest sensation that his head was rolling away from him.

Maybe if he sat up.

He placed his hands in the snow and, with a series of short jerks, pushed himself up against the branch. When he eased back, he felt pressure at the base of his skull.

He squinted, but the chaos buoyed his stomach, and he shut his eyes.

He was quiet then. He listened to the laughter drop on him from out of no where. And then, slowly, his mind seemed to fade, to pass from him.

But then he heard the voice.

The compass, it said.

The voice, his father's, came from inside and outside his head.

"Wha'?" He pressed against the snow with his elbows, straining to hold his eyes open against the riotous motion.

The compass. Give it over.

"I know wha' you wan'," he said belligerently. "You doan gotta tell me."

Where is it?

"Keep yer shir' on! Can' you tell nothin'? Ah, chrise, whatsa use. Shoulda known not to 'spect nothin'. Nah from you. Here!" And with that he forced his hand inside his shirt. The sheer weight of his arm popped the top two buttons. He felt along the lanyard and touched smooth metal, then closed his hand and squeezed. It felt far away.

Throw it at him. That's what he'd like. Why did he have to come like this, for the compass and not for him?

He squeezed, trying to crush the hard, round object, but there was no give and, finally, he eased his grip and clumsily drew his hand out. He opened his fingers and, looking down his nose, tried to focus, but the object raced away in a short arc, stopping and then jumping back, only to race off again. He closed his eyes. Still, he was sure he had seen gold, not silver.

"It's nah the compass," he said, raising his head and laughing. "Itsa watch. Well whaddayah know? The gahdamn wash." He gripped his forehead, trying to stop the feeling that his head was rolling away. He chuckled. "Wha' in hell did I do wiffa compass?" He remembered something. What?

Breaking it. That was it. He'd broken the compass. By accident. And then... and then on purpose. Atta boy.

It's in your vest, he heard his father say in the instant that he remembered himself.

In his vest... In his vest pocket. He shook his head. Was that right? Yes, yes. Now he remembered.

It's in your pocket.

"I know, damn it! I know where it is for crisesake!" He waved his father off defiantly, his right arm shooting forward, out of control, dropping into the snow. With stops and starts, he brought his hand back and felt for his pocket.

Broken. Wait till he saw.

He straightened a little and pushed his hand into his pocket and, when he felt the compass, he laughed, laughed long and loud.

"Ha-ha-ha!" and he pulled his hand out. "Loooo-look." He opened his hand, resting it heavily on his thigh. "Go 'head. Loooo-look!"

Then his hand slipped into the snow, palm up, but he did not drop the compass.

"Whatsa matter, Pa? Come on, taye the damn thing, it's so, pre-precious to you. Taye it!"

He lifted his head and, raising his hand, tried to spit, but his mouth was dry, hardly capable of making a spitting sound. A moment later, his arm grew so heavy he had to rest it in his lap. He rubbed his thumb against the casing, rubbing it in and out of one dent, fast and hard.

And then his father laughed, harshly, and, when he heard the harshness, he felt tears. They came in a rush. He bit his upper lip and tried to hold it in, but his mouth burst, and he sucked a coughing breath into his lungs. It went out again, shaking.

"Oh, Pa," he cried. "Why wasn't it me you came bah for?"

He covered his mouth and pressed hard with his left hand.

"I 'member," he said, dropping his hand. "The nigh' you gave me this. God, I din wanna take it. I'd've given it back. Given it baa so fast. And afferwards... I thought..."

He drew a breath, his chest tightening and choking.

"It's jus' tha'... I thought... ah thought you hated me so... I coon help b'lievin' that you... din wan' me ta come out. Nah ever. That's why the map wuss wrong, so I never come out..."

He clamped his hand over his mouth and pressed hard. Then he tried to lie quiet, his hand falling into the snow.

In awhile, he felt neither warm nor cold, just wrung. And then he felt a great heaviness moving into him. Startling, he tried to push it off with his left arm. It swiped the air and dropped into the snow. The heaviness moved deeper.

He felt cold against his fingers. It reached his mind like a sound heard in sleep that takes a long time to touch consciousness. He raised his hand and, after a miss, touched his wet, cold fingers to his lips. Then he started and came off the branch, shouting: "Pa, doan leave me!"

His eyes shot open, but he could not focus. The heaviness was pressing, pushing him back against the branch. His hand was on the snow, but it felt so far away.

I'm sorry, Pa. Never wanted to hate you. But too much. Trying so hard. Hoping just once you'd say I was good enough.

He wiped one eye with his fingers, smearing his cheek.

Trying so hard so maybe you could love me. Finally realizing it was too much... And then, then hoping maybe you could just stop hating me. Could stop blaming me for her.

He let his head loll, and he exhaled in one long, shaking breath.

"Four, an' you nevah tole me it wassa lie." It was a whisper.

He cried quietly, in little squeaks. He snuffled.

"Gone... So I coon even tell her I was sorry. B'lievin' she mus' blame me too. Papa woon lie. He woon.

"Good, god, and Jim, too!" His head came off the branch. Then he settled, moaning.

Never hated you. Just once. You were leaving, too. And I hadn't ever said I loved you. And I hated you. 'Cause you were going, and hadn't said it either. Then it was too late. I'd done it, and it was too late. Was sorry. Wanted to take it back. But how?

His eyes were closed, and the heaviness pushed into him. He was looking through his eye lids, and he could see the sky. It was all gold and black, the clouds piling into the heavens. It was the most beautiful sky he had ever seen. Then the heaviness withdrew.

He swallowed, and snuffled, and twice more licked his lips.

I never hated you.

"Wha'? Wha'?" He tried to push against the branch, but the heaviness moved deeper and pressed on his eyelids, making them heavy. He wanted to sleep.

I never hated you. Never wanted you dead.

"Wha'? Wha', Pa?"

Sometimes, boy, you ain't got the brains you was born with. 'Course the map was wrong. Any jackass can follow a map. Woodsman's gotta be different. You had to face what was in you. Know that you was better'n it. Didn't I tell you that?

"Wha'? Yeah, once, Pa. You tole me."

How many times I gotta repeat a thing?

He licked his lips so he could answer, but his tongue stuck.

What about my note? You find it?

He tried to nod.

What more you need?

He wanted to believe. So sleepy, though. He lifted his hand, trying to signal he understood. His hand was so heavy. The heaviness pushed into his chest. There was the feeling of barrel hoops tightening around him.

Light. Moving, dancing against his eyelids.

A fire?

Yes, a fire, with his father on the other side, his face bright like a moon against the darkness, but then fading, with a smile just breaking on his lips.

"Pa!" His eyes shot open, but he could not rise. A great, smothering inertia pressed him down again.

I never hated you.

Yes, yes.

The tightening around his chest grew fierce, suddenly releasing and tightening again.

He forced open his eyes, just a slit against the overwhelming heaviness. His father was still there, white and brown against the mountains, his arms spread. He went back against the branch.

"Buh did you evah luff me?" he muttered.

Then he could hear his father laughing. It was such a strange laugh. It seemed to fall on him from high above. It stopped.

So tired now. So sleepy.

You think I didn't? he heard his father say from inside his head, outside his head.

He scarcely nodded.

Boy, you denser than a brick. Would I have spent all them years teaching you if it was otherwise?

The question came to him slowly, seeming not to be spoken, but to rise out of the muck of memory.

Would I have shared my woods with you, the thing I cared for most?

Would I have given a good goddamn if you ever learned to face up to yourself?

Didn't figure it needed to be said.

He rolled his head, uncomfortable from the creeping heaviness. He could hardly breathe.

Say it then.

No! Ain't going to say it. Ain't one for fawning.

It's true?

'Course it's true.

True?

Damn it. I said so!

Yes, you said.

You satisfied?

"Yeh. It'sa 'nough. 'Nough. Mayes me glad. Sorry, too. So sleepy now, Pa."

Don't got to be sorry.

His mind was working slowly, thoughts moving as if through honey.

The compass, Pa...

The thoughts came so slowly.

Take it.

He raised his right arm, barely strength enough. His arm swung away from him, but his father quickly caught his wrist, a distant, wooden touch.

He waited, but his father did not pry his fingers open.

So it was his? His!

Go home now, Pa? You and me.

He listened.

And then his father's harsh laughter tumbled out of nowhere, distant and fading, so he knew he had started back.

You got your own ass into this mess, he heard his father say from far off. Now you can just get it out again, too.

The voice was receding, but playful, joking. And then there was more laughter.

His old man. He was something... out here.

He had to follow...

He tried but could not move.

It didn't matter. Too sleepy. Father wasn't moving. He could hear him laughing. Joking him. He was sure something. He'd sleep; then he'd follow the laughter home.

He heard the wind moan somewhere far off. And then he felt it blow through him and out again into the white and trackless wilderness, taking the heaviness as it left, just as the compass loosened and slipped from his hand.

ABOUT THE AUTHOR

James A. Naughton grew up in North Adams, Massachusetts, surrounded by the Berkshire Mountains and the forests that still exist there. In his youth, he was a hiker and backpacker. He did not fully appreciate, until he left North Adams, just how deep and indelible a stamp the Berkshires and the wilderness of western Massachusetts had left on his life. He received a graduate degree from Northeastern University and a post graduate degree from the University of Connecticut. Retired now, he worked more than 30 years as a writer in the life insurance and investment management industries in Boston.

Made in the USA
Middletown, DE
10 October 2016